CHERIE DIMALINE

THE MARROW THIEVES

DCB

Canada Council   Conseil des Arts
for the Arts   du Canada

ONTARIO ARTS COUNCIL
CONSEIL DES ARTS DE L'ONTARIO
an Ontario government agency
un organisme du gouvernement de l'Ontario

Canadian   Patrimoine
Heritage   canadien

Canada

The publisher gratefully acknowledges the support of the Canada Council
for the Arts and the Ontario Arts Council for its publishing program.
We acknowledge the financial support of the Government of Canada through the
Canada Book Fund (CBF) for our publishing activities, and the Government of Ontario
through the Ontario Media Development Corporation, an agency of the Ontario
Ministry of Culture, and the Ontario Book Publishing Tax Credit Program.

LIBRARY AND ARCHIVES CANADA CATALOGUING IN PUBLICATION

Dimaline, Cherie, 1975–, author
The marrow thieves / Cherie Dimaline.

Issued in print and electronic formats.
ISBN 978-1-77086-486-3 (paperback). — ISBN 978-1-77086-487-0 (html)

I. Title.

PS8607.I53M37 2017   jc813'.6   C2016-907292-4
                                              C2016-907293-2

Cover photo by Wenzdae Brewster
Cover design: angeljohnguerra.com
Interior text design: Tannice Goddard, bookstopress.com
Printer: Friesens

Printed and bound in Canada.

Manufactured by Friesens in Altona, Manitoba, Canada in October 2018.

United States Library of Congress Control Number: 2016945346

DCB
AN IMPRINT OF CORMORANT BOOKS INC.
260 SPADINA AVENUE, SUITE 502, TORONTO, ON, M5T 2E4
www.cormorantbooks.com

For the Grandmothers who gave me strength.
To the children who give me hope.

"The way to kill a man or a nation is to cut off his dreams,
the way the whites are taking care of the Indians:
killing their dreams, their magic, their familiar spirits."
— WILLIAM S. BURROUGHS

"Where you've nothing else,
construct ceremonies out of the air
and breathe upon them."
— CORMAC MCCARTHY, THE ROAD

FRENCHIE'S COMING-TO STORY

MITCH WAS SMILING so big his back teeth shone in the soft light of the solar-powered lamp we'd scavenged from someone's shed. "Check it out." He held a bag of Doritos between us — a big bag, too.

"Holy, Mitch! Where'd you get that?" I touched the air-pressurized bag to confirm it was real. My dirty fingers skittered across the shiny surface like skates. It was real. My mouth filled with spit, and a rotten hole in one of my molars yelled its displeasure.

"In the last house back there, hidden on top of the cupboard like Ma used to do when she didn't want us getting into stuff."

Mom had only been gone a few months, so talking about her still stung. My brother popped the bag to cover our hurt. And like cheese-scented fireworks, that loud release of air and processed dust cheered us up.

We were in a tree house somewhere on the outer rim of a small city that had long been closed down like a forgotten convenience store. We were a few hours out from Southern Metropolitan City, which used to be Toronto back when there were still so many

cities they each had a unique name instead of a direction. West
City, Northeast Metropolis, Southern Township ...

It was a great tree house; some lucky kid must have had a
contractor for a father. It was easily two storeys up from the
unmown lawn and had a gabled roof with real shingles. We'd been
there for three days now, skipping school, hiding out. Before
he'd left with the Council and we never saw him again, Dad had
taught us that the best way to hide is to keep moving, but this
spring had been damp; it had rained off and on for over a week,
and we couldn't resist the dry comfort of the one-room tree
house with built-in benches. Besides, we reasoned, it was up high
like a sniper hole so we could see if anyone was coming for us.

It probably started with that first pop of air against metallic
plastic, no louder than a champagne cork. I imagined the school
truancy officers — Recruiters, we called them — coming for us,
noses to the wind, sunglasses reflecting the row of houses behind
which we were nestled in our wooden dream home. And sure
enough, by the time we'd crunched through the first sweet, salty
handfuls, they were rounding the house into the backyard.

"Shit."

"What?"

Mitch put the bag down and turned to the window cut into the
north wall.

"Francis, you're going to have to listen to me really carefully."

"What?" I knew it was bad. He never called me Francis, no one
but Mom ever did, and then only when I was in trouble. I'd been
Frenchie since I could remember.

"Listen, now." He turned away from the window to lock eyes
with me. "You are going to climb out the back window and onto
the roof, as low down as you can get."

"But, Mitch! I can't climb out a window."

"Yes, yes you can, and you will. You're the best damn climber there is. Then when you're on the roof, you're going to grab the pine tree behind us and climb up into it. Stay as close to the trunk as you can. You have to shimmy into the back part, where the shadows are thickest."

"You go first."

"Too late, buddy; they know someone is up here, just not how many someones."

I felt my throat tighten to a pinhole. This is how voices are squeezed to hysterical screeching.

"Mitch, no!"

He turned again, eyes burning with purpose, bordering on anger. "Now. Move it, Francis!"

I couldn't have him mad at me; he was all I had left. I clambered out the window and folded upward to grasp the slats on the roof. I shimmied up, belly to the wood, butt pulled down tight. I lifted my head once, just high enough to look over the small peak in the center, just enough to see the first Recruiter lift a whistle to his mouth, insert it under his sandy moustache, and blow that high-pitched terror tone from our nightmares. Under the roof I heard Mitch start banging the plywood walls, screaming, "Tabernacle! Come get me, devils!"

Fear launched me into the pine. The hairy knots on the sticky trunk scraped my thighs, sweat and skin holding me there. The needles poked into my arms and shoved into my armpits, making me tear up. I pulled my sweaty body towards the other side of the pine, scrapes popping up red and puffy on my thighs and torso. All the while the whistles, two now, blew into the yard.

"Come get me, morons!"

I saw both of the Recruiters now: high-waisted navy shorts, gym socks with red stripes pulled up to their knees above low, mesh-sided sneakers, the kind that make you look fast and professional. Their polo shirts were partially covered with zip-front windbreakers one shade lighter than their shorts. The logo on the left side was unreadable from this distance, but I knew what it said: "Government of Canada: Department of Oneirology." Around their necks, on white cords, hung those silver whistles.

Mitch was carrying on like a madman in the tree house. Yelling while they dragged him down the ladder and onto the grass. I heard a bone snap like a young branch. He yelled when they each grabbed an arm and began pulling. He yelled around the house, into the front yard, and into the van, covering all sounds of a small escape in the trees.

Then the door slid shut.

And an engine clicked on and whirred to life.

And I was alone.

I wanted to let go. I wanted to take my arms off the trunk and fold them to my chest like a mummy, loosen my thighs from their grip, and fall in a backwards swan dive to the bottom. I pulled one hand back and clutched the opposite shoulder. *Deep breath. You can do this.* The other hand shook as it began to release. The skin of my thighs burned with the extra strain. Soon they too would be unclenched. Deep breath …

If I survived the fall, which was possible, I'd be taken to the school with Mitch. This thought was appealing at first, and for a brief moment I had some kind of TV reunion in my head: me, Mitch, Mom, Dad … but I knew that's not how it would go. A few had escaped from the schools, and the stories they told were anything but heartwarming.

"THERE'S A MAN named Miigwans who came by Council last night," my father had said one night when we were still together. "He escaped from one of the satellite schools, the one up by Lake Superior." Dad had bags under his eyes. He'd gathered us around the kitchen table to talk, but spoke haltingly, like he'd rather not. "He told us about what's happening to our people. It wasn't easy to hear, and was he frantic, tried to leave right away, looking for this Isaac fellow."

"Jean, maybe the boys should go in the other room for this ..."

"Miigwans says the Governors' Committee didn't set up the schools brand new; he says they were based on the old residential school system they used to try to break our people to begin with, way back." He paused and drank half the liquid in his greasy glass, a kind of moonshine he kept in an old pop bottle on the back stoop. He placed it hard on the picnic table we'd hauled into the main room of the cabin. The glass echoed the wood in its hollow curve. It was punctuation. It made me jump. He was in the gloomy place he went to when he spoke about how the world had changed. He said we were lucky we didn't remember how it had been, so we had less to mourn. I believed him.

"Okay, boys, that's it, off to bed." Mom shooed us off the bench, pushing us out the door before we could formulate an argument to stay. Dad stopped me to kiss the top of my head, and I felt safe, even just for a minute.

We heard Mom crying as we lay in bed that night. And the next day, we packed up that small cottage we'd been staying in since our apartment in the city had lost power and things had gotten dangerous. We hadn't even spent a full year there, and none of us were keen on leaving, especially me and Mitch. We had family here, blood and otherwise. There were other families, people

like us, who had settled here. The old people called it the New
Road Allowance. And now we were jamming clothes and jars of
preserves wrapped in blankets into our duffel bags to move again.
I thought about our walk into this settlement from the city.

"We walk north," Dad had said then. "North is where the
others will head. We'll spend a season up by the Bay Zone. We'll
hole up in one of those cabins up there and I'll try to find others.
We'll find a way, Frenchie. And up north is where we'll find home."

"For sure?"

"Hells yes, for sure. I know so because we're going to make
a home there. If you make something happen you can count on
it being for sure."

"What will we find up there, Dad?" I'd been nervous it would
be all empty and wet, the constant rain making pools in our
footprints before we could completely empty them of our feet.

I was tired and hungry, and my shoes were as thin as cardboard,
but I tried not to let any of that color my voice when I spoke. I knew
we were all tired and hungry and trudging along on leather-skin
shoes. I knew to be positive in that way that a little kid comes home
from school and can tell there's been an argument that day by the
way the air smells in the front hall and decides this is the day he'll
start his math homework without being asked. Survival, I guess.

We were out by old Highway 11, having slipped the noose of
the last suburb of East City. Unlike the smaller city outskirts where
I'd later lose my brother, these suburbs were open and vast, a maze
of darkened windows and burnt cars in kaleidoscopic boroughs
that branched out like a geometric blossom of asphalt and curb
and erupting driveways.

I'd felt kind of special then, before I knew how dangerous
special could be. I guess I was proud of my family, with our ragged

shoes and stringy hair; we were still kings among men. I held my twiggy walking stick like a scepter, chin tilted towards the ashy sky.

And now here we were again, getting ready for another journey into another unknown, driven by fear. But we never made that move, not together, anyway. At what was supposed to be my father's last Council meeting before he took his family north, it was decided they'd make one last-ditch effort to talk to the Governors in the capital. They never came back.

I KNEW I'D never see my family if I were captured; we wouldn't be reunited at the school. I had to get down from this tree safely and keep moving. Mitch had sacrificed himself so I could live, so I had to live. It was the only thing left I could do for him.

I pulled myself back against the tree, hugging the craggy trunk so hard I had tectonic imprints on my cheek and thighs for three days after. I stayed there until the van drove off, until I couldn't hear the engine anymore, until the day filled up with grey, until the grey turned indigo. Then I shook each sleepy limb, each screaming muscle back into service and half slid, half climbed back down the tree to the ground. The landing vibrated into my shins and set my kneecaps loose like baby teeth. I sat there a moment before the memory of the shrill siren of the Recruiter's whistle shoved under my feet like slivers. I was almost to the house next door before I remembered to turn back for my backpack and the half-eaten bag of chips.

The first night I kept going, running when I could, crawling against every surface that offered a shadow. I even pissed on the run, dribbling on my duct-taped boot. The morning after, when I was truly alone in the bright of day, I was all panic and adrena-

line. I found a rain barrel behind a small detached bungalow at the
end of a cul-de-sac somewhere by the outlet mall and drank as
much water as I could, then right away threw most of it back up.
At least my boot was clean again.

Here the sidewalks were shot through with arterial cracks
and studded with menacing weeds that had evolved to survive
torrential rain and the lack of pollinators. Wildlife was limited to
buzzards, raccoons the size of huskies, domestic pets left to run
feral, and hordes of cockroaches that had regained the ability
to fly like their southern cousins. I had been scared of them all
when I was still running with my brother. Now, in the wake of
his removal, they were nothing. I crunched over lines of roaches
like sloppy gravel, threw rocks at the pack of guinea pigs grunting
at me with prehistoric teeth from under their protective awning
at a corner grocery.

"No one cares, you little shit!" I screamed at the largest male,
who stood his ground on the outer perimeter of the awning,
stomping his boundary on surprisingly muscular front legs like
some kind of caricature of an old bulldog. Behind him huddled his
nuclear family, a circle of two smaller females and about eighteen
bucktoothed guinea pig children.

"We're all dead anyway. I should make a shish kebab of your
kids."

I didn't mean it. I looked at their round eyes, wet and watching
but not nervous enough for the threat of a human. Their dad
was there, after all, and they knew they were safe. I felt tears
collecting behind my own eyes like sand in a windstorm. I opened
my mouth ... to say what? To apologize to a group of wild guinea
pigs? To explain that I hadn't meant what I'd said? To let them
know I just missed my family? A small sob escaped instead.

I cupped a dirty hand over my mouth to catch it, but not before the male smelled my fear and turned his back to me. I was no danger to them. I was no danger to anything. At best, I was prey.

It was early evening when I hit the edge of the trees. According to the small plastic compass clipped onto the zipper of my backpack I was now heading northeast. Dad had said we should head north to the old lands. We'd told mom we were heading east when we lost her at the seniors' home. I figured northeast was the safest bet.

Now I was alone, leaving the smaller cities that had winked out long ago like Christmas lights on a faulty wire. The trees here were still tall, so I wasn't very far north, but they were dense, so I wasn't too south anymore, either.

My legs screamed from a night and day of ache and stretch marinated in old adrenaline and scabbed with tree bark cuts. I collapsed under a pine. It was still spring, and I knew the night would be too cold for a single boy with no real shelter other than a thermal wrap and a couple layers of hoodies. The early moisture would set in, and I couldn't afford to get sick. So I built a modest fire just big enough to cut the chill and lay on my back, backpack under my head.

Out here stars were perforations revealing the bleached skeleton of the universe through a collection of tiny holes. And surrounded by these silent trees, beside a calming fire, I watched the bones dance. This was our medicine, these bones, and I opened up and took it all in. And dreamed of north.

Cold is an effective alarm clock, and I was up before the sun. The fire had gone out, but not long ago, since there was still smoke. The cough I'd been cultivating over the past few days was more insistent now. I coughed, and each push of air brought a fresh ache out of my back and legs. The jump and the run had really done a number. Still, I stood and started my jumping jacks, following Mitch's morning warm-up routine even though he wasn't there to motivate me.

"C'mon, French. I've seen higher from a boulder!"

I rolled up my sweaters and the wrap and jammed them in my backpack before a quick breakfast of the second to last tin of meal replacement drink and a granola bar with a bite already missing. My stomach grumbled when I finished, but there was maybe a day and a half of food supplies left in my pack and I was heading into the woods. There'd be no grocery stores or abandoned duplexes to raid for leftovers and non-perishables. I wasn't quite sure how I would do it. Mom had said her uncles and grandpa were great hunters, that it was a family trait. Maybe it would just come to me, like a blood memory or something. What would I even kill an animal with, a stick?

I started back north, keeping my eyes to the ground for animal tracks with no idea of what I would do if I actually saw some, or if I would even recognize what animal made them.

By the time the sun reached center stage, a punctuation mark in the cloud-lined sky, I was miles into the woods. The trees were denser, the ground less manageable, and the wildlife — judging by the sounds and smells around me — had changed. I stopped in a small clearing filled with tall grasses and low bushes. It was the thud of my heart against the hollow bowl of my stomach that made me eat a cluster of dandelion weeds grown to waist height. They weren't bad. I added them to my "available and edible" list and clomped on, the plastic compass pressed into my palm now like a toy talisman. I kept trudging north.

"YOU HAVE TO try to keep the goal in your head. You can't let what's not here, what's missing, you can't let that slow you down." Mom was trying hard to give us a pep talk on top of the seniors' home in a small city on our last night as a trio. But with a monotone voice and that far-off look she'd taken on since Dad had left with the lost Council, it was hard to take in the message. Her words fell in between the sheets of rain like downed planes: defeated, useless.

"Mom, here." Mitch held an open can of artichoke hearts he'd just grilled with a lighter. "You need to eat."

She ignored him. "There were generations in our family where all we did was move. First by choice, then every time the black cars came from town and burned out our homes along the roadside. Now the cars are here again. Only now, they're white vans. And I can't run that fast. Not fast enough. Never fast enough."

"Mom," Mitch spoke louder but still gently. I was huddled against the side of the gazebo, peering through the wooden lattice, on the lookout for Recruiters. "You haven't eaten all day. You need to eat."

Her eyes stayed fixed, away from her eldest. The smell from the lake here was nauseating. Once this was a popular city, being right on the water. Now this lake, like all the industry-plundered Great Lakes, was poison, and a tall fence blocked it off from the overgrown streets. We hadn't been here more than a day, so the smell was pungent for us. We breathed into bandanas and built shelter from the stench with plywood and a tarp.

Mitch tried a different tactic with Mom. "If you don't eat you won't have the strength to take second shift tonight."

Something flickered on her face and she reached out, removed one pale heart from the cluster, and inserted it into her mouth like a chore. It was a few minutes before she spoke again.

"We have to move, my boys. Tomorrow we move, after I do one last forage in the old Friendship Center."

"Mom, no! That place is a hot spot for Recruiters. It's a pretty obvious Nish-magnet."

She squinted her eyes. "Oh now, the officers are long done with that place. There's no Indians left in this part of the city anyway. I'm just going to look for a few things we'll need once we get past the city and into the bush. It'll only take me a minute." She reached for our hands and squeezed them, breathing deep and full like a prayer, chewing her bottom lip like penance.

The next day she left before we reheated artichoke for breakfast. And then Mitch and I were on our own.

I WAS STUMBLING. Another night asleep in the open. This time I didn't have enough strength to rebuild the fire that had been rained out while I fitfully slept. My muscles ached, my belly rumbled, my heart hurt. I'd tripped over an aboveground root bent like an arthritic finger and picked up a limp. The rain started again just after noon, and I sat under a dense pine nursing my last tin of meal replacement, the last-resort tin with the expiry dated for the previous year. There was a sour current through the frothy top notes, but it was all that was left; I hadn't even seen any more damn dandelions. My molar screamed every time a swallow of liquid passed over it. Just this morning I had started contemplating dentistry with a rock. Or maybe I could just fall out of a tree, cheek first. I fell asleep biting a piece of shoelace, leaning against the pine trunk, wishing Mom would find me.

A shiver woke me up. It was almost full dark, and my tooth

hurt and my ankle throbbed and I'd spilled what was left of the tin on the ground beside my legs.

"Oh no." I righted the tin and shook it. Not even a mouthful left. "Damn it!"

I tried to throw it into the woods, to make that damn tin pay for my own carelessness. It arched up and hit the ceiling of pine branches above me, slamming back to the ground not a foot in front of me. I kicked it instead.

"Jesus!" My ankle sang a terrible song like my toothache had sunk to my foot. Rot and damp and hopelessness and hunger and fear and anger twisted up in a clamp around my ribcage.

I sat back down, picked up the can, and rubbed it across my greasy forehead, back and forth, back and forth. No one to take care of me now. No one to make me move. Where the hell was I going anyway? Where the hell was my mom? Why did she have to go to the Friendship Center? Her eyes that night: hollow like an old stump. Like the hole in my molar, a true ache.

"I'm going to die."

Saying it out loud was like hearing it from another person's mouth. It made my head well up with tears. I held onto them; precious water. I decided then that if I was going to die, I wasn't going to sit there and wait for the truancy dicks to come get me. I'd die fighting wild animals, or swan diving from one of these pines, or of starvation half buried in the drying earth like a partially cremated corpse floating down the old Ganges, before the Ganges became a footpath for heartbroken pilgrims.

I stood back up, dropped the can, and shouldered my pack.

Onward.

I fell a couple of times, tripping over roots sticking out from ground that was ashy and loose in the thinning earth, washed out from the endless rain. I split my lip on the last tumble and tasted wet pennies and heavy perfume. *Shoulda turned my head to hit my tooth*, I thought. I laughed out loud, a desperate sound that made me laugh harder so that I had to stop, hands on my shaking knees, and wait out the wave of giggles that made it impossible to trudge on.

The cough was near constant, stiff and phlegmy like a sack of bricks slamming against my insides. It made me double over and drool. I broke a blood vessel in my right eye with the hack. The walk was slow with sickness and the limp. I didn't even notice my stomach had pulled itself into a fist until I was being punched by it, nauseous and cold. And now, night was falling.

"Nooooo." I couldn't do anything to protect myself from it, so I whined. "Shit, no."

I leaned against a knobbly pine sticky with sap that matted the back of my head to the bark and watched the sky betray me into navy. I slid then, slow and painful, ripping out my hair so that a clump of me stayed pinned to the tree — nesting material for low-flying buzzards. The stars began to rip through the hard skin of dark like the sharp points of silver needles through velvet. I watched them appear and wink and fade, and I smiled. This wasn't going to be so bad. Maybe the end is just a dream. That made me feel sorry for a minute for the others, the dreamless ones. What happened when they died? I imagined them just shutting off like factory machines at the end of a shift: functioning, purposeful, and then just out.

I closed my eyes. Just for a minute. The dream came for me right away. Later, I couldn't recall what it had been or for how long I'd been asleep. But when I woke, it was reluctantly.

"PUT HIM DOWN over there, right close to the fire."

"He's breathing all funny."

"Never mind now, just prop up his head. Wab, go grab that quilt from my bedroll. Zheegwon, heat up some water. We'll need to get some liquid into him."

Voices. Voices with the pulled vowels and cut lilt of my father. Voices with the low music of my mother. I couldn't open my eyes. Not yet. This was too beautiful a dream, even just in audio.

"All right now, pull off his shoes and get his feet close to the pit."

I felt tugging and then the relief of a good swell allowed to spread out, then heat.

"Hey, boy, can you hear me? You'll need to drink some of this water." A metal edge split my broken lips and clear, warm water poured into my mouth. I sputtered at first, a reaction to the intrusion, then the fist in my guts demanded it and my throat opened up in compliance. The need was so great, the satisfaction so complete, I grasped for the vessel, lest it be pulled away.

"Easy now, easy now."

I managed to open one eye.

There was a man holding the tin, not my father, but a man with the same crease around his eyes. His hair was long down the middle and shaved close on the sides. He looked to be about my father's age. Over his right shoulder a girl stared at me with one round, dark eye, her long hair draped around her face, flickering in tandem with the flames of the large fire. She handed a blanket to the man, who tucked it in around me.

"Zheegwon, get some soup over here. This boy is starved."

The man spoon-fed me broth with sweet corn mush until the fist unclenched just enough for me to rest, then he put it beside me on a flat rock. "When you can hold it yourself, that's when you know it's okay for you to eat more without getting sick."

I opened both eyes and looked around. There were more people now. There was the man, and the older girl who'd brought the blanket, who I saw was wearing an eye patch and had an angry red slash down her cheek. There was a child, not much older than a baby, sleeping in a nest of blankets like a puppy beside an old lady dozing in her kerchief. Then there was a small, round boy, two taller boys who looked like they must be twins, and another tall boy whose face was hidden by the shadow of a hood. They all sat around a roaring fire on blankets and sleeping bags and they seemed to all be Native, like me. Behind them were two canvas tents shut tight against the cold air and the new bugs that had found the blood around my mouth interesting.

"Who are you?" It wasn't more than a whisper.

It was the man who answered, standing to poke at the branches in the fire. "I'm Miigwans, and this is my family. But not now. There'll be time for that tomorrow. You need to eat some more of that soup and then sleep. Tomorrow we move. Probably got some Recruiters nearby with the racket you were kicking up by yourself out there."

Miigwans. I'd heard that name before. I could see my father's mouth pronouncing it with reverence, like he did for everything that had a touch of the old about it, the words from our language; like a prayer.

"North."

He turned his face to me, flames animating the shadows that fell there under his eyes, along his cheekbones. "Yeah, that's right, north. We seem to be heading in the same direction. Might as well trudge on together then, eh?"

I didn't answer. The tears cleared away the dirt from my eyes, stinging as they crossed my split lips. Sobs rocked me, open and closed, until I was fetal. I was embarrassed to be so broken in front of all these new Indians. If they were embarrassed for me, no one made a motion or mouthed a reproach. They just let me be broken, because soon I wouldn't be anymore. Eventually, I wouldn't be alone, either. And maybe tomorrow I'd wake up and find myself closer to home.

THE FIRE

MIIG EXPLAINED IT one night at the fire.

"Dreams get caught in the webs woven in your bones. That's where they live, in that marrow there." He poked at the crackling wood with a pointy stick till the shadows were frenetic against his tan face, till they slid into the longer shoots of hair near the front of his mohawk, the tendrils he swept up and patted into place atop the shorter brush with the care of a pageant queen. He didn't make eye contact with us, the motley group seated in a loose semicircle around the fire, beneath the trees where he commanded place.

I imagined spiderwebs in my bones and turned my palm towards the moon, watching the ballet of bones between my elbow and wrist twist to make it so. I saw webs clotted with dreams like fat flies. I wondered if the horses I'd ridden into this dawn were still caught in there like bugs, whinnying at the shift.

Miig nudged the rounded stones placed around the perimeter of the fire with his boot. You could see where the holes in his sole had been patched up with sap and scavenged leather.

"How do they get in there?" RiRi, now seven, was always curious and not shy with her questions.

"You are born with them. Your DNA weaves them into the marrow like spinners," Miig answered. The flames tried to settle, and he prodded them to dance again. He added, "That's where they pluck them from."

I pulled each one of my fingers into my palm and made a fist silhouetted against the fire, flames licking around the tight ball of brown and bone. I imagined my brother tied to a chair at the school, a flock of grey-hooded villains tightening his beaded chains while they recited Hail Mary like synchronized swimmers.

Miig sat, satisfied that we were all at attention, that we were listening with every cell. He leaned against a felled tree beside Minerva, who woke up with his rustling. He rolled a smoke out of his precious tobacco stores and plucked a twig out of the fire with a burning ember at the tip to light it with. Old Minerva, near-sighted to squinting, lifted her nose at the smell. Her lips fell slack and she sighed. Those first few exhales were big and wasteful as Miig tried to get the damp paper to light, and smoke billowed across the clearing like messages. Everything was always damp, so we were trained to sniff out mould to keep that sickness at bay. Minerva made her hands into shallow cups and pulled the air over her head and face, making prayers out of ashes and smoke. Real old-timey, that Minerva.

Miig and Minerva were the only grown-ups in our group. Miig wore his hair shaved to the skull except down the middle and had a moustache that only grew on the left side of his top lip. He was tall but bent like a walking question mark, and he was short with words and patience. Miig wore army pants, alternating between two identical pairs, and layers of brown and green sweaters.

He kept a small pouch hung on a shoelace around his neck and tucked into those sweaters. Once, when I'd asked him, he'd told me that was where he kept his heart, because it was too dangerous to keep it in his chest, what with the sharp edges of bones so easily broken. I never asked again. Too many metaphors and stories wrapped in stories. It could be exhausting, talking to Miig.

Minerva was dark, round, and tiny like a tree stump. She kept her long grey hair in two braids like a little girl with a flowered kerchief tied over her head and under her round chin. She had old-timey ways, but you couldn't get much from her, either. She didn't talk, and when she did it was in bursts accompanied by laughter and maybe a scream or two. Mostly she watched … everything: us kids playing in the river, the way the trees tilted to the north towards what was left of the natural landscape beyond the clear-cuts stripped of topsoil. She watched the birds on their perpetual migration to anywhere, the fire at end of day, and the way we clapped each other's backs when trading off on the traplines.

There were seven of us in the group: five boys and two girls, not including the Elders. Not one of us was related by blood, which was a good thing for those closer in age, since, in the old days when our families were huge and sprawling, accidently dating a second or third cousin had meant you had ask about genealogy right off the bat. But it was also lonely, not having the common connection of grandparents or aunties like we used to have so often. There was Chi-Boy, who at seventeen was the oldest boy and taller than anyone else. He was quiet almost to the point of being mute and as skinny as a doe. He never seemed to sleep as long as the rest of us or need as much food, and he stuck close to Miig so that when he was needed he was no more than one syllable away. He came from the west, from the Cree lands.

After Chi-Boy there was me, sixteen. I was nicknamed Frenchie as much for my name as for my people — the Metis. I came from a long line of hunters, trappers, and voyageurs. But now, with most of the rivers cut into pieces and lakes left as grey sludge puckers on the landscape, my own history seemed like a myth along the lines of dragons. Compared to Chi-Boy's six-plus feet, I wasn't the tallest, but I did have the longest hair of any of the boys, almost to my waist, burnt ombré at the untrimmed edges. I braided it myself each morning, to keep it out of the way and to remind myself of things I couldn't quite remember but that, nevertheless, I knew to be true. My clothes were also burnt from the sun and wear, a mottled brown from their original tones of black.

Then there were the twelve-year-old twins, Tree and Zheegwon, whose matched green eyes communicated without words between them. They were broader than the rest of us, with wide shoulders and heavy hands that hung from ropey arms. They were dotted with scars I couldn't bring myself to ask about. They shared one baseball cap between the two of them, changing it from head to head, one day to the next.

Slopper was next, the nine-year-old with the belly of a fifty-year-old diabetic. His family came from the East Coast.

The girls had Wab, who at eighteen was practically a woman. She had a vicious keloid slash that split her face nearly in two. Then there was RiRi, who came from a Metis community close to where my father had said ours used to be, who was old enough to piss in the bush and swear when we played Red Ass on abandoned brick walls, but who was still a child.

Us kids, we longed for the old-timey. We wore our hair in braids to show it. We made sweat lodges out of broken branches dug back into the earth, covered over with our shirts tied together at the buttonholes. Those lodges weren't very hot, but we sat in them for hours and willed the sweat to pop over our willowy arms and hairless cheeks.

"It's time for Story." Miig exhaled smoke as he spoke. I watched the word *Story* puff over the fire and spread into a cumulative haze that smelled of ground roots and acrid burn just above our dark heads.

Slopper struggled to his feet and started over to his tent. The youngest weren't privy to Story, not yet anyway. RiRi made the face she pulled out when she wanted something, like an extra piece of camp bread or to sleep in my tent so I could tell her stories to keep the nightmares away.

Miig just looked at her, lifting one eyebrow higher than the other.

"Aww, Miig. Can't I stay for a little bit?"

She received no answer, and kicked rocks all the way to her tent.

The woods grew quiet now; even the beetles stopped rubbing their smooth shells on softened bark, even the wind picked around the branches instead of rattling straight through.

Miig leaned in so that the fire illuminated his face from the bottom like unsteady stage lights. And he opened a hand, palm down to indicate the ground, this ground, as he began Story.

STORY: PART ONE

"ANISHNAABE PEOPLE, US, lived on these lands for a thousand years. Some of our brothers decided to walk as far east as they could go, and some walked west, and some crossed great stretches of narrow earth until they reached other parts of the globe. Many of us stayed here. We welcomed visitors, who renamed the land Canada. Sometimes things got real between us and the newcomers. Sometimes we killed each other. We were great fighters — warriors, we called ourselves and each other   and we knew these lands, so we kicked a lot of ass."

The boys always puffed out their chests when Miig got to this part. The women straightened their spines and elongated their necks, their beautiful faces like flowers opening in the heat of the fire.

"But we lost a lot. Mostly because we got sick with new germs. And then when we were on our knees with fever and pukes, they decided they liked us there, on our knees. And that's when they opened the first schools.

"We suffered there. We almost lost our languages. Many lost

their innocence, their laughter, their lives. But we got through it, and the schools were shut down. We returned to our home places and rebuilt, relearned, regrouped. We picked up and carried on. There were a lot of years where we were lost, too much pain drowned in forgetting that came in convenient packages: bottles, pills, cubicles where we settled to move around papers. But we sang our songs and brought them to the streets and into the classrooms — classrooms we built on our own lands and filled with our own words and books. And once we remembered that we were warriors, once we honored the pain and left it on the side of the road, we moved ahead. We were back."

Minerva drew in a big, wet sniff, wiped her nose across her sleeve, and then set about chewing the fabric once more.

"Then the wars for the water came. America reached up and started sipping on our lakes with a great metal straw. And where were the freshest lakes and the cleanest rivers? On our lands, of course. Anishnaabe were always the canary in the mine for the rest of them. Too bad the country was busy worrying about how we didn't pay an extra tax on Levi's jeans and Kit Kat bars to listen to what we were shouting.

"The Great Lakes were polluted to muck. It took some doing, but right around the time California was swallowed back by the ocean, they were fenced off, too poisonous for use."

I'd seen the Great Lakes: Ontario when we were in the city and Huron when we lived on the New Road Allowance. The waters were grey and thick like porridge. In the distance, anchored ships swung, silent and shuttered, back and forth on the roll of methodical waves.

"The Water Wars raged on, moving north seeking our rivers and bays, and eventually, once our homelands were decimated and the water leeched and the people scattered, they moved on to the towns. Only then were armies formed, soldiers drafted, and bullets fired. Ironically, at the same time rivers were being sucked south and then east to the highest bidder, the North was melting. The Melt put most of the northlands under water, and the people moved south or onto some of the thousands of tiny islands that popped up out of the Melt's wake across the top of our lands. Those northern people, they were tough, though, some of the toughest we've ever had, so they were okay, are still okay, the tales tell. Some better than okay. That's why we move north towards them now."

Miig stood, pacing his Story pace, waving his arms like a slow-motion conductor to place emphasis and tone over us all. We needed to remember Story. It was his job to set the memory in perpetuity. He spoke to us every week. Sometimes Story was focused on one area, like the first residential schools: where they were, what happened there, when they closed. Other times he told a hundred years in one long narrative, blunt and without detail. Sometimes we gathered for an hour so he could explain treaties, and others it was ten minutes to list the earthquakes in the sequence that they occurred, peeling the edging off the continents back like diseased gums. But every week we spoke, because it was imperative that we know. He said it was the only way to make the kinds of changes that were necessary to really survive. "A general has to see the whole field to make good strategy," he'd explain. "When you're down there fighting, you can't see much past the threat directly in front of you."

"The Water Wars lasted ten years before a new set of treaties and agreements were shook on between world leaders in echoing assembly halls. The Anishnaabe were scattered, lonely, and scared.

On our knees again, only this time there was no home to regroup at. Meanwhile, the rest of the continent sank into a new era. The world's edges had been clipped by the rising waters, tectonic shifts, and constant rains. Half the population was lost in the disaster and from the disease that spread from too many corpses and not enough graves. The ones that were left were no better off, really. They worked longer hours, they stopped reproducing without the doctors, and worst of all, they stopped dreaming. Families, loved ones, were torn apart in this new world."

He stopped suddenly, the fire bouncing over the planes of his face, something so sad it hurt to look in his eyes. And then the rain started again. He couldn't continue. Couldn't walk us into the darker parts of Story, not now.

"Enough for tonight, then."

We packed up what lay about while the fire still burned. Carrying the tarp we used as a dining room table over to the tents, I heard her call.

"French?"

I sighed and dropped my shoulders, still smiling. "Yeah, Ri?"

"Can't sleep."

This was fast becoming the routine. I heard Story, she did not. So she would ask me to tell her stories, innocently enough, but desperate for some understanding, the understanding that was withheld from her youth so that she could form into a real human before she understood that some saw her as little more than a crop.

"Be there in a minute."

"'kay."

I pegged the tarp between RiRi's and Minerva's tents so that they'd have a little covered walkway should they have to use the washroom during the rainy night. I carried over the cleaned latrine bucket and a smaller bucket half filled with water for washing up. Then I took my boots off at the door and joined RiRi in her tent. Until last month she'd shared a tent with Minerva. But she was getting older and had demanded some space, which was granted. We encouraged independence in our family. We never knew when anyone would be on their own, even at seven.

The tent was small, and the firelight from outside made everything the same red as the vinyl walls. She had made a nest of her blankets in the middle on top of her blue ground tarp, away from the walls that could hold condensation and spread dampness in a good enough downpour. I lay down beside her on top of the blankets. Her pillow was like all of ours, a case stuffed with folded clothes. There was no room for extras in the camp; everything did double duty.

Before I'd even laid my head down, she was after Story.

"Tell me what happened, French. Please."

"Ri, you know I can't tell you."

"But why? Why can't I know?" She lifted herself up on an elbow, pleading. "It's no fair. I get sent away all the time!"

I rolled over onto my back, reaching up to tap the raggedy dream catcher I'd bent out of branches and filled with vines for her so that it swung on its string. "It's for your own good."

She squinted at me in the red gloom. "That's a load of bull. I deserve to know my own history."

It was getting more difficult to reason with her, especially when she made sense. RiRi had been just a baby when I'd joined the camp, newly walking and bucket trained. For some reason she quickly grew attached to me. Miig thought I must have reminded her of someone from her original family. Whatever the reason, I often had a chubby shadow throughout my day. Now that she was a real kid with her own duties and her own mind, it was becoming increasingly hard to relegate her to the shadows and to ignore her requests for information, for background to her difficult life.

"Ri, Slopper was allowed to hear Story when he was younger," I began.

"What?! That's no fair!" She was up on her knees in a flash. "How come he got to hear?"

"Relax, relax." I pushed her shoulder, trying to get her to lie down. "Listen to me, please."

I stopped talking until she grudgingly lay back on her side, facing me. "Slopper was allowed to hear Story a couple years ago, when he was your age. He didn't even hear it all, and it didn't turn out so well."

"But I'm not Slopper, French." She had sprung back up. "I can handle it. I'm mature for my age."

I laughed at this. "I know that's true, Ri. You're practically a grown-ass lady."

She pursed her lips, checking my face for mockery. When she found none, she gave me a stiff, "Thank you."

"But it's about timing. Miig will let you know the whole story when it's time. Slopper was pretty messed up for months after. He stopped playing, didn't want to learn anything, and even stopped sleeping so good."

She was finally quiet.

I watched the dream catcher spin to a stop. I remembered following Mitch around, bugging him for any details he might know as we tromped after my parents to the Bay. I thought about the parts Miig had left out tonight, the parts that kept us running. Even still, it was unfair to keep everything from Ri. It had driven me to distraction to not know, made it harder to keep moving day after day without understanding what was on our heels.

"Maybe ... yeah, I think maybe I can share some things, though." Her eyes grew big, but she held back her words.

"Years ago people, other people, not us, they kinda got sick. Really the whole world itself got sick." I tiptoed around the harsher images that came to mind. "Like, it never used to rain all the time. And there were way more people.

"After the rains started and the lands shifted so that some cities fell right into the oceans, people had to move around. Diseases spread like crazy. With all this sickness and movement and death, people got sad. One of the ways the sadness came out was when they slept. They stopped being able to dream. At first they just talked about it all casual-like. 'Oh, funniest thing, I haven't dreamed in months.' 'Isn't that odd, I haven't dreamed either.'"

Here I pitched my voice high and wiggled my shoulder to imitate a mincing kind of movement, like how I imagined white ladies did as they pushed metal carts down long straight aisles to gather food from boxes lined up on shelves, all of it already dead. RiRi smiled at this impression.

"They visited their head doctors — psychiatrists — and they took pills to help them sleep when they stopped having the will to lie down at night. Soon they turned on each other, and the world changed again."

A low whistle with a fluttering end sounded outside. The alarm. I jumped up.

"Where are you going?" RiRi sounded frantic. She'd just started to hear Story and now I was leaving.

"Gotta go. Something is coming." I dashed out of the tent, stepping into my boots with the laces still undone.

The rest of the group, with the exception of Slopper, was around the low fire.

Miig acknowledged me with a look and then sought out Chi-Boy with his eyes. He motioned with his head to the east of our site, keeping in a crouch and hurrying to the trees. We were out in the open, it was too late to run or hide, we'd have to fight. Chi-Boy pulled his long blade out from the sheath where it hung at his belt and backed into the trees until the shadows covered him completely. I needed to help. I grabbed a long stick from the fire, its end glowing with orange heat scales, and waited. My hands shook so the stick clattered a bit against the rock perimeter of the fire. Wab had crept over to crouch in front of Minerva. She nodded at me, and I scanned the forest behind them. Sweat dripped down the bridge of my nose. I blinked as if that would relieve its slow, maddening itch. Then I heard it.

Footsteps in the bush. Not heavy steps, light and cautious. Just like a Recruiter on the prowl. I raised the stick behind me like a bat, pulling it up and over like a sword. I could hear the sizzle of the lit tip by my ear.

Closer.

I swallowed hard and almost coughed, catching it at the last minute so that my eyes teared over. I heard Miig owl call to Chi-Boy, who answered with deep silence.

Closer.

The steps were slow but steady. I picked up the swoosh of a drag, like a bag or maybe a body. Maybe we weren't the first camp to be discovered. I could swear I saw the branches move in the trees, just past the second row beyond our clearing.

"Come on, goof. Come and get it," I whispered, tossing my weight between the balls of my feet, trying to be brave.

Closer.

Now I saw Miig, sidestepping between the first and second rows, his feet silent in their patched-up shoes. Why was he out in the open like that? Maybe he was playing decoy? Should I start rounding up the others to run? My breathing got louder, and the footsteps stopped.

Shit! Could they hear my fear? Did I give us away?

"What the hell?!" A high-pitched yell and then, two seconds later, Chi-Boy emerged, dangling a girl by her forearm from his height.

"Let go of me!"

She was spinning and kicking and I'm pretty sure spitting. Chi-Boy pulled her out of the shadows and dropped her in front of the fire, a foot from where I stood with the dry stick raised behind my head. Miig emerged next with a large green duffel bag.

"Jesus holy God! You scared me!" She was angry. Her eyes swung around the circle, taking in the fire, the tents, and the people. Then she found me.

"And what in the hell are you doing, posing for a goddamn Hall of Fame statue?" She rubbed her arm where Chi-Boy had held her.

Miig carefully put her bag by her feet and took a few steps back. I lowered my stick and speared the ground over and over.

"Some welcome." She glared at us.

When I lost enough adrenaline to notice the way her cheeks held shadows but her eyes were clear, one thought jumped into my head.

Please don't let her be my cousin. Please …

MAGIC WORDS

ROSE HAD BEEN with us for about three weeks before she fully settled in, putting up her tent beside ours, sharing food without suspicion, and even laughing this big, throaty laugh she had that filled all the space. And although she hadn't shared her coming-to story yet, I knew enough about her to know we were not blood related. Thank God, because she made me feel like I needed to be a better person just through her existing.

She was a fighter and became more vocal about it every day. We were used to her outbursts during Story; in fact, she became part of Story, the dissenting voice to the way things are, the rebel waiting for the fight to be brought. And we loved the way she rebelled, anyway; having been raised by old people, she spoke like them. It made us feel surrounded on both ends — like we had a future and a past all bundled up in her round dark cheeks and loose curls.

IT WAS A beautiful night, in that time of year when the bugs go to sleep, so we stayed together by the fire instead of zipping into our tents. Rose was moody and made a sudden declaration into the quiet: "We should go after the government arseholes ourselves, no more running. " She threw her hands out. The fire made the shadows of her fingers into a huddle of people against the trees. Old Minerva watched the new shadow people, slowly clapping her hands at their firelight jigging.

Miig poked the fire. "We've survived this before. We will survive it again. Trust that there is always someone who has taken the greater good as mission." Miig squashed his dying smoke under his heel and stretched out his legs, making a pillow between his head and the log with his hands.

Beside him, Minerva was now beginning to snore, her head slumped to a shoulder, a ball of string clutched in her hand. Rose sat back down, and we slowly placed our limbs into sleep positions under the wide, wide sky.

"Someone better come up with a plan soon, by the Jesus. Or I'll make one." She said it more to herself than to any of us. I watched her, her eyes deep and reflective, her lips moving with whispers about action and the people and all the damn world itself. I'd never seen anyone who looked like Rose before. She said she got her looks from having a Black father; her small, wide nose; her dark, severe bones. I think it had more to do with her stubbornness and the way it got caught up in her eyebrows and dimples when she was over-thinking something. When she closed her lids over those mirror eyes, I turned to the woods and invited the dreams in, hoping they'd include the last face I memorized in profile.

"YOU BOYS NEED to work on your hunting."

"But there's, like, no animals around here, Miig."

Miig put his hands on his skinny hips and sighed, shaking his head down as he exhaled. "Doesn't matter. They'll be back, and you need to be ready. 'Sides, maybe if you were better at hunting you'd catch one of the dozen or so animals that are around here." He was addressing Slopper, who kicked rocks with the toe of his beat-up Converse.

We stood in the trees in a circle around Miig, who was loading his gun while he gave us the charge for the day. We did this every second or third day, depending on the weather; sometimes it was hunting, others it was shelter-building. Miig said it was Apocalyptic Boy Scouts. We didn't know what in the hell he was talking about, but we liked fashioning bows and arrows and whooping to each other through the bush and feeling all Chiefy. We took turns, splitting into groups, Hunting and Homestead, switching off every three months. The Homesteaders were back at the campsite packing up for the next slide northward and watching Minerva, who had been braiding RiRi's hair and tapping out a tune on the top of her head in pauses when we left them.

We were lucky; we had Miig to learn from instead of Minerva to babysit. We clamored out of the camp, all elbows and bravado, feeling our superiority, owning our luck. Rose, her massive curls tangled on her head in a sloppy bun, shot me a look from the tent she was dismantling, having been stuck with Homesteaders. I watched my feet navigate the tripwires we'd set up yesterday and avoided her disdain.

"You got to know how to tell animals are nearby. How would you do that? Anyone?"

Slopper's hand shot up, exposing his round belly hanging out the bottom of his shrinking t-shirt. All of our clothes got worn to dust. It was rare to come across anything out here, and even if we did, you had to wear the new boots or holed sweater a few weeks before you forgot a dead man had worn it. I had lucked into a pair of fleece-lined army pants two winters past. They had been frozen to a low branch where someone must have left them to dry. I rolled them three times on each leg and kept them up with a rope for forever. Just this season I'd finally been able to let them hang to their full weight. Because I had pants and a coat and even gloves with only two fingers worn to skin, all clothes we found were passed on to the others. Soon enough I would be looking for new pants and the goods would go my way first.

Miig tried not to sigh, but he did, a little. "Yes, Slopper?"

"You see them?"

"Okay, Slopper, if they're close enough for you to see them, there better already be a bullet or an arrow on the way to take them down. Anyone else have any ideas on how we can track them to get close enough to shoot?"

Chi-Boy answered. "Ground marks."

"Okay, like what?"

"Shit." My face got hot when the others laughed.

"That's right, Frenchie. If you see shit on the ground, you know the asshole who dropped it must be close by."

Miig's response brought fresh peals of laughter, including my own.

"You can also tell by its, err, freshness, how long ago the animal was at that spot. Anything else?"

We spent the morning talking and looking at examples of trees gored by shedding antlers and branches snapped by lumbering bodies. Wab led us through the brush, trying to demonstrate the movements required to take prey by surprise. It was after midday when we began the walk back to the camp with a couple of rabbits and one patchy-furred squirrel for lunch before an afternoon march to the next bunking.

I was walking with Slopper and Chi-Boy. We were singing a song we'd made up to an old-timey round dance double beat. Chi-Boy had a beautiful high voice, and when he sang he squinted his already small eyes to slits. It made him look like the friendliest giant in the forest. I loved watching him sing. Slopper hammed it up a bit, trying to mimic and trying to pretend that wasn't the case.

Way ya, hey ya, hey ya, way ha
I don't know where we're going
Don't know where we've been
Way hey ya
All I know is I'll keep walking
Can't get taken in
Way hey ya

We sang it around and around in our warbling voices somewhere between youth and where they would settle, like bees around a single flower. We were delirious with it, tossing the chorus back and forth between us like a ball, making up new lyrics as we grew bored with the old ones.

Miig was oddly quiet. Usually at about the sixth time through he'd snap at us to shut it. But today he just kept two paces ahead. He didn't even yell at the twins for lagging behind to pick up interesting-looking rocks for their growing collection. "Maybe you should collect feathers instead of rocks. It's not the smartest collection when you're on the run," he'd told them more than once.

I jogged up to meet his pace. "Hey, Miig, what's up?"

He kept cadence and didn't answer for a full minute. "Birds are too quiet."

"Maybe they went ahead."

"But why?"

We came into the camp from the east, stepping over the wires and ducking under the hanging bells. The Homesteaders had almost everything ready for the move, stacked and tied in one pile. There was just a dinner fire glowing and the people themselves, sitting on the fallen logs we'd dragged around the pit like they'd been waiting all day for our lazy arses to get back. I searched the faces for Rose. When I found her, I looked away and then just happened to stumble over to her log to sit.

Miig handed the catch to Wab. As the only woman in the bunch, other than crazy old Minerva, the management of the cooking fell in her domain. Not that she had to cook everything herself, just that she got to say who did it and how. As the woman of the group, she was in charge of the important things. Even though she'd hunted that day, she decided to take care of things herself. Wab gathered her long bleached hair into a ponytail, looked us over once with her small, dark eyes, and then set about skinning the animals on a flat rock with her beloved blade. She liked this solitary work, her fingers catching and releasing, pulling and knotting in old rhythms, especially after having to mentor the Hunters.

I felt Rose on the log beside me. It's like the shape of her body heat fit right into me and I couldn't ignore her for long. "I feel bad for you guys."

"What? Why?" Rose was all aggression out of the gate. She turned to look at me, her curly hair wild around her round face, half tucked into her too-small parka.

"Well, because we get to go learn from Miig and you guys are stuck with that." I pointed with my lips across the fire to Minerva, who was absorbed in chewing through a bag of porcupine quills she'd harvested last week when we ran across its carcass. "I hate when it's my turn for Homesteaders. It's so useless."

"Stuck with Minerva? Huh, you have no idea." She leaned forward, her elbows on her thighs. Our knees were almost touching.

"As bad as that, eh?" I commiserated, glad to have something to talk about, glad that she leaned into me to do so.

"No, not bad at all. As a matter of fact, being with Minerva is pretty nishin." She narrowed her eyes.

Uh-oh. "Nishin? What in the hell is that?"

"Oh nothing, just a little of the language."

I jumped up. "Bullshit!"

She jumped too, throwing her shoulder into mine. "Not bullshit. Real shit."

"How do you have language?" My voice broke on the last syllable. My chest tightened. How could she have the language? She was the same age as me, and I deserved it more. I don't know why, but I felt certain that I did. I yanked my braid out of the back of my shirt and let it fall over my shoulder. Some kind of proof, I suppose.

She pushed her face into mine, and for the first time I didn't think about kissing her. I didn't notice then, but would recall later, that she had cut bangs into her hair that day, that they fell a little lower on the left side and she had to brush them out of her eye.

"Minerva. Minerva has the language and us poor guys are stuck with her so we learn." She used her fingers to put air quotes around *poor guys*. Then she used those same fingers to push me in my chest.

I had to turn away. I had to walk out towards the perimeter of the clearing, into the darkness of branches and shadow. Because I wasn't sure if I was going to cry or scream, and I didn't want her to witness either.

"Hey, Frenchie, don't go far there. We need to get some rest now. We're heading out at first light." Miig called me back to the fire. I hunkered down into my sleeping spot as soon as we finished our meal, before even the first stars ripped through the black.

Nishin. Nishin. Nishin.

I turned the word over in my throat like a stone; a prayer I couldn't add breath to, a world I wasn't willing to release. It made my lungs feel heavy, my heart grow light, until the juxtaposition of the two phased into sleep.

I COULDN'T YELL, had no voice to make noise with. All I could do was watch and shake my head from the tree while down below on the overgrown lawn Mitch waved up at me all happy and carefree. Behind him six Recruiters crept forward in a semicircle, trapping my brother between them and the dense trees in which I was hiding. I pleaded with him with my eyes. I had to hold on to the trunk with everything I had; I knew that if I didn't I'd fall and Mitch would be angry. I tried to lift one hand, just one hand so I could point to the Recruiters, now barely six feet away, but as soon as I loosened a finger I started to slide and Mitch's face grew dark. I had to. I just had to. I couldn't let them take him again.

I pulled my left hand free and started pointing like crazy. Mitch was upset, and he called to me. "No, Frenchie! Hold on, for God's sake. Hold on, Frenchie! You hear me?"

"FRENCH. FRENCHIE." SOMEONE shook me awake with the toe of their boot. "Get up, we gotta go now."

I woke up sweating, Zheegwon standing over me, his brother, Tree, slightly behind him. They'd hit a growth spurt this past summer. It made their almost consistent silence a little more intimidating. My sleeping bag was wedged between my legs in a sweaty twist of polyester and anxiety.

"Yeah, okay." I wiped the sweat from my eyes and sat up. Kids were already shouldering their packs. Miig was pouring water on the pit. I took a piss in the bushes and rolled up my gear fast.

"Let's go. We need to make ground today." Miig's eyes were squinty, and we moved faster than our usual pace. Minerva and little RiRi were relieved of their baggage to give them a bit of an advantage so they could keep up. A seven-year-old and a thousand-year-old need as much of an advantage as they can get, I suppose.

We had walked for almost an hour before I felt the last fingers of the dream loosen from my lower back. The sun was warm this morning even as we edged further north and further into the season.

"It means good."

It was Rose. She'd caught up to me, even with the added weight of RiRi's roll attached to her own with a fraying bungee cord.

I looked at her, a question in my eyes.

"Nishin. It means good."

I kept my eyes on the trail ahead. I didn't mean to, but I said it anyway. "So?"

"Sooooo," she said. "If you want to know what Minerva tells us, I'll share."

I took three strides before I could answer. "Okay."

"Okay?"

"Yeah, okay."

She punched my arm. I couldn't help but smile. I wanted to say her name, to feel it rumble past my teeth.

"Yeah, Rose. That sounds nishin."

HAUNTED IN THE BUSH

FOR A WEEK I'd had trouble sleeping. I wanted to see Mitch and my parents when I closed my eyes, but not in the way they had been coming to me as of late: Mom showing up in my tent with her mouth sewn shut and her left arm missing; Dad sitting by the fire drinking out of a Mason jar, then jumping into the flames when I got close enough to smell the moose hide of his mitts. I spent a lot of time with RiRi, and she took full advantage of my resistance to sleep.

"Where did you walk from?"

"The outer city."

"Did the Recruiters chase you?"

"They would have. My brother stopped them."

"Did your brother get taken?"

"Yeah, Ri. He got taken."

"What did he look like?"

"He seemed really big, but I don't think he was. I think maybe he was just always bigger than me. He had eyes that were blue sometimes but sometimes looked grey. And his hair was almost black. His teeth were crooked so that the front ones looked like they were holding hands."

It was painful, but I didn't really mind. The more I described my brother, my parents, our makeshift community before Dad left with the Council, the more I remembered, like the way my uncle jigged to heavy metal. Instead of dreaming their tragic forms, I recreated them as living, laughing people in the cool red confines of RiRi's tent as she drifted off.

I woke up with stiff muscles and frozen toes on her tarp one morning, her small form huddled under layers, cheeks pink with warmth and rest. I must have fallen asleep in the middle of talking the night before. I could see my breath and hear the near constant rain pattering on the vinyl walls. A slow, steady drizzle. That's the best we could hope for these days. Miig couldn't explain the science of it, but ever since the North started melting there were more rains.

I shook the damp out of my legs and laced my boots back on, wrapping the tops in strips of fabric that tore as I knotted them. Almost time to replace them. Thank God I was done with the last growth spurt. I'd ended up having to wear flip-flops for weeks; they were the only thing that fit until we scavenged a forgotten fishing lodge and found the boots I wore now.

Outside, Wab and Chi-Boy were already packing up her tent. She moved away from him when I came out, and he shuffled off to fold up his own tent, leaving her to wind the rope and store her pegs. Something about their movements, choppy and stilted, made me feel awkward. I tried to fill the space with words.

"Good morning. Uh, hey, Wab, start breakfast yet?"

"Twins are on meal duty. They're Homesteaders."

"Oh right. I forgot it was hunting day. Yippee, more squirrel and mushroom stew."

She didn't answer. Instead she gave me a wry look, then started braiding up her hair as she watched Chi-Boy work.

"Not that I don't like your stew, it's just ..."

Thankfully, I was interrupted when Slopper farted loud and long from his tent. We couldn't help but laugh.

"Christ! Sounds like that one ripped a hole in the ground," one of the twins shouted from the main latrine behind a dense thicket. Chuckles could be heard from Miig's and Minerva's tents.

"Gross." Ri was up.

With that introduction to the new day, the camp came to life, one by one: brushing their teeth with brushes worn to stiff nubs, beating the wet out of clothes by slapping them against trunks, and running tight circles around the perimeter to warm up.

We sat in a quiet circle, packing our gear and waiting for food. The Hunters strapped on the wristwatches we shared. Miig didn't need one; he kept a pocket watch in his jeans. It was important for Hunters to keep time, so we could keep track of each other and the day.

"We never used to need these things," Miig commented as we wound the mechanisms and checked they were synchronized. "But no one has the skill of telling time by the sky here. Maybe one day we'll run into someone who does. Then we won't have to rely on these things no more."

The twins opened a few tins of condensed milk, handing the empty cans to Minerva, who rinsed them out in a puddle. She smiled while she cleaned the lids and pulled them off, stashing them in the leather cross-body bag she wore every day. Who knew what she was up to. Minerva collected odd things. We didn't even question it anymore. Miig crushed the tins as small as they could go so we could bury them along with our other minimal garbage by the latrine.

After a hasty breakfast of mush, the Hunters were off, eager to take advantage of the halt in the rain and the appearance of sliced sunlight through the striated clouds.

"It is often necessary to break up a larger group to achieve a goal, especially since a lone shadow can get into more spots without notice than a larger group." We were a fifty-minute hike from the camp.

"I want you all to get used to the idea of operating alone." Miig was crouched down in the middle of our huddle, checking the ground for fresh prints. "There're signs of deer in this area, maybe something bigger. If we work separately but together we should bring back a nice buck."

"Woohoo!" Slopper pumped his fist in the air, being a huge fan of fresh deer meat.

"But only," continued Miig, looking at the excited boy, "if we can stay quiet and focused."

Slopper lowered his fist and shuffled his feet.

Miig stood, put his hands on his lower back, and stretched. "We are going to each go our separate ways. So make sure you keep track of which direction you walk. Cross twigs on the paths when you change directions to find your way back without tipping off potential predators. And have your weapons ready."

Chi-Boy and Wab were carrying bows. Slopper, not having graduated to full Hunter status, carried a sharpened stick. Miig had his .45, and I had the rifle slung over my shoulder. Chi-Boy used to carry the rifle, but he and Wab had been spending time relearning bow hunting, so it fell to me now.

"Bows are sustainable. Eventually we won't be able to get more bullets, and at least I can make arrows," he'd explained. I think they just liked having this thing they shared in common, never mind all the hours it provided them alone to practice.

"Everyone goes a different way. Keep a steady but mindful pace, the same speed we keep on the trail when we move camp. An hour's walk, no more, then you find a lookout and wait." Miig reloaded his handgun and tucked it back in his waistband. With his long raincoat with the popped-up collar and the .45 in his wide leather belt, he looked like an old-timey gunslinger. "We wait for two hours, then make your way back here. If there's a problem, you all know the alarm. Chi-Boy?"

Chi-Boy threw his head back and let out a screech that curved up into a tail before fading. An eagle.

"Okay?"

We all nodded then turned and pushed off into the bush like swimmers from the block.

I walked southeast, careful to pace my steps so that I was moving neither too fast nor too slow to keep the group synchronicity that would make it easier to track anyone who didn't return on time. Just in case. Our lives were a series of actions twinned with "just in case" reactions.

The ground was cold and soggy. I could feel it through my boots. The earth barely had a chance to absorb the rainwater before the next deluge. It hadn't been this bad even when I was on the move with my parents and brother. Every year the world was making us more aware of change. After the cities crumbled off the coastlines, after the hurricanes and earthquakes made us fear for a solid ground to stand on, even now we were waiting for the planet to settle so we could figure out the ways in which we would be safe. But for now there was just movement, especially for us: the hunted trying to hunt.

I concentrated on my gait, marking the changes in direction, following nothing but the way my feet seemed to divine. I made up goals as I walked to pass the time: if I avoided snapping even one twig in the next five minutes, it meant I would stop ten minutes early; if I could remember the names of Mom's three favorite books, I would rest for three minutes ... Even if I did manage to stay quiet, and even if I did remember the books, I still walked on.

At fifty-nine minutes, thirty-two seconds, I stopped, pulled my lighter hunt bag and the rifle off my back, and settled into the nook made by a felled tree. I pushed up into the guts of its roots where they had been yanked out of the ground. The hole it left had filled with filthy water, but the roots were dry and tangled enough to make a comfortable seat.

I climbed up into the middle of the roots and leaned back. It was kind of soothing like that, with a dozen wooden knuckles massaging my back. I leaned my head into the mess, limbs dangling with no effort, just another set of roots protruding out of the fallen tree. I exhaled and paid attention to the way my lungs sank in, with just a little bit of rattle at the end left over from my annual bronchitis.

My mind wandered. I tried to keep it focused on my surroundings, but I was tired and so I let it run a bit off leash for lack of the energy to remain disciplined. From where we were now, running, looking at reality from this one point in time, it seemed as though the world had suddenly gone mad. Poisoning your own drinking water, changing the air so much the earth shook and melted and crumbled, harvesting a race for medicine. How? How could this happen? Were they that much different from us? Would we be like them if we'd had a choice? Were they like us enough to let us live?

I thought about the sickness and the insanity that crept like bedbugs through families while they slept. What would I have done to save my parents or Mitch, given the chance? Would I have been able to trap a child, to do what, cut them into pieces? To boil them alive? I shuddered. I didn't want to know what they did. And I didn't really want to know if I'd be capable of doing it.

Time passed. I may have fallen asleep once or twice. The world out here was quiet, like the land was holding its breath. But if you listened, really put conscious action into listening, things began to sing. Insects with wings pirouetted somewhere above my prone head. From the hole where the tree had once held on to the earth came the sound of deep movement, maybe just the mud shifting. And a group of small birds chatted with some clipped formality in the pines on the other side of the clearing. And then there were footsteps.

I lifted my head, flexing my arm to raise the rifle into position.

Soft shuffling over by the pines. I aimed the gun, watching the trees, praying for nothing more than a deer, nothing human, really.

It was huge, like a tree had yanked itself up and was slowly moving into the clearing, a tree with bone white branches. It walked further into the grass. A moose. I'd never seen one this close before. Adrenaline made my teeth chatter.

Time is slow in that vacuum space. In this new space, I had time to aim squarely between the moose's eyes, watching his muscles contort and his skin wrinkle as he bent to take another mouthful of grass. Then I decided against it, lowering the barrel to his chest: always go for the sure target. Miig had taught us that on one of my first hunts, and I listen to my Elders.

Just then he raised his head, so massive I wondered at the blood it must take to animate, and he saw me. He blinked a long, slow blink and faltered for only a second or two before he began chewing again. He turned a bit so that I knew he knew I was there. I swallowed hard, aiming, fingers exact and stiff. He was so frigging big. It was like he was a hundred years old, like he had watched all of this happen. Imagine being here through it all — the wars, the sickness, the earthquakes, the schools — only to come to this?

He exhaled, long and loud like the wind. This was food for a week. Hide and sinew to stitch together for tarps, blankets, ponchos. This was bone for pegs and chisels. This was me, the conquering hero, marching into camp with more meat than all of us could carry, taking the others back to field dress this gift. This was Rose looking at me with those big eyes so dark they shone burgundy in the firelight. This was my chance.

But could we travel with this meat before it rotted? No. And could we smoke and dry it? No, Miig wouldn't set up camp for that long, especially not with a steady thread of smoke reaching above the trees, blasting a signal to anyone who might be out there. So we'd be leaving half, at least half, behind to rot.

The moose watched all this play out on my face, a dirty boy tangled in the roots of an upended tree, hiding from the world, hiding from memories of a family and days without pursuit. And he stayed perfectly still. His eyes were huge, dark globes that reflected back their surroundings. I was sure I could see myself in there, in the trees, a long-haired warrior taking aim.

I lowered the rifle. He blinked once more, then crossed his

legs, one over the other as if at the start of a curtsey, then turned back into the trees.

I couldn't do it. I couldn't let it come to this, not for him and not for me.

Walking back to the meeting point, I swung between peace with my decision and wrenching regret. I was empty-handed, but something in my chest was burning a little brighter. I was okay with my decision, but not okay with the consequences. I secretly hoped no one else had gotten anything so I wouldn't be the only loser, even if it meant we went hungry for a day. I pictured RiRi's face, sad because of an empty belly. That made me ashamed.

As it turned out, I didn't have to worry about RiRi. When I made it to the meeting spot, Chi-Boy and Miig were already there, each with a wild turkey strung up in the lower branches of a maple.

"Grabbed mine in the first twenty minutes. The rest must have been scared off by the shot and headed towards Chi-Boy there. He grabbed one too." Miig was laughing, enjoying a hand-rolled smoke.

Slopper was napping, leaning against a log.

"No luck, French?"

Watching them pat each other on the back and proudly spin their turkeys, examining the carcasses for size and weight, I was back to wrenching regret.

"Nope. Nothing."

Chi-Boy glanced at his watch. "Ten past."

"She'll be here." Miig scanned the area. "She's good."

Miig told the story of his turkey and rolled a new smoke to replace the one he'd finished. Slopper was awake now, yanking out a few of the nicer feathers from Chi-Boy's bird. Chi-Boy didn't protest; he was pacing the perimeter, looking at his watch.

"Twenty-five after."

"Boy, give her another ten and then we'll start off in her direction." Miig was sympathetic but short. "She's fine. Better out here than most of us."

We'd almost hit the ten-minute deadline when Wab silently slipped in beside us. Chi-Boy sighed, and even smiled. But he made no movement towards her. She was empty-handed, which was weird for her, not that it bothered me. Misery loves company, I suppose.

"Everything okay?" Miig's forehead wrinkled at her expression. She nodded. "Let's head back."

Without another word, she led the way back to camp. She didn't tell us what she'd seen out there until it slipped out a week later.

A PLAGUE OF MADNESS

IN A WAY, I got that moose. He visited me in my dreams. I was walking along the sandy shore of Huron, the surface brown and healthy, and there on the other side, beside a weeping willow that dipped the tips of its branches into the water, stood the moose. He wasn't watching me, but I knew he knew I was there. Another time, I was walking through the bush, my right hand outstretched against the cool brick of a building buried deep in the trees. I followed the wall straight for a mile until it turned the corner. I walked around the corner, and way down this side, which seemed to go on for another mile, was the moose, blocking the path between the brick and a dense thicket of bush. I started walking towards him. I woke up before I reached him, fingers already anticipating the soft warmth of his flank.

It was a calmer time for us. There hadn't been a Recruiter sighting for weeks, and we settled into a more leisurely pace. We enjoyed this new cadence, taking the time to help Chi-Boy gather sticks for arrows, playing in the clearings dotted with strangely robust flowers new to the territory. Only Wab seemed stressed.

She rushed ahead when we took our time. She was the last to fall asleep, walking the perimeter of the camp and double-checking the wire alarms. She ate little and said even less. There was no real way to figure out what was wrong; Wab was prickly on the best of days. So we stopped asking her to join our games and stopped offering her the best cuts of meat. She wouldn't take them anyway. Her mood stayed the same for days, until one night at the fire, after Minerva and the younger kids and the twins had wondered off to bed, she asked a question: "Do you think circumstances make people turn bad? Or that people make circumstances bad to begin with?"

Miig exhaled a long plume of smoke. "Well, that's not an easy question."

Rose walked over from her tent, having grabbed a sweater and returned to the circle, sitting between me and Wab. Chi-Boy and I stared into the flames of the dying fire, waiting for the old man to continue. I was surprised to hear her talk after such a long silence and wanted to engage, but if anyone could address her question, it would be him.

"I read this book once, written by this Algerian fellow. Camus was his name." He examined the heater on his smoke, packing it in and trimming the ashes by dragging it on a rock by his feet. "Anyway, in this story was all these people trapped inside their own town because the plague attacks them and they are put into quarantine."

I'd never heard this story before. But I knew what a plague was. That's what they were calling the dreamlessness when it started, a plague of madness.

"So these people, they start to change. Some of them, like the doctor, stay close to the same because he gives everything he's got — his time, his expertise, his clinic — to working for the people. But I guess that's change too, just closer to his real nature."

"So, we change because of circumstances. But if you're a good person, you change in a good way?" Wab sought to cut to the message right away.

"Well now, not necessarily." He stubbed out the butt and popped the remainder in his pocket to roll into the next one. "I think it's more like you do what you need to in order to keep yourself intact. It's about motivation."

"Like how we are motivated to run because of the Recruiters?" Rose jumped in. "And the Recruiters are motivated to run after us because of the schools?"

"Almost," he answered. "We are actually both motivated by the same thing: survival."

"But isn't it just us that's trying to survive? No one's trying to kill those jerk-offs."

"But, nevertheless, they are dying. Mostly killing themselves, mind you. And so they are motivated by the need to be able to survive. And they see that solution in us."

Wab was on her knees now, listening so hard she was leaning towards each speaker. "So, we're the same?"

"In a way."

"So then I'm right. If we're both motivated by the same thing, and they are the ones hurting people, then that's their nature, they're bad to begin with."

Miig steepled his hands and paused before he asked, "What would you do to save us?"

We looked at each other, faces bright in the singular light of the fire. We were family. We were all we had. The rest was dark and unknown.

It was Chi-Boy who answered. "Anything."

Wab spoke after him. "Everything."

Rose reached across the space and put her hand on mine. I grabbed it and laced our fingers together.

"Exactly. We all do what we can to survive. Right now, they can chase us. And us? We can run. It may not always be this way, and who is to say what we will be capable of."

We were quiet for so long, Miig began to stand up, pushing his hands on his thighs when Wab spoke again.

"I saw men in the woods."

Miig sat back down. We waited.

"When we were on the hunt last week. Two of them." She looked up at us. "And I knew one of them."

Chi-Boy slid closer to her. "Who was it?"

She shook her hair. "Someone who wasn't very honest. Someone from my old life."

Chi-Boy got uncharacteristically gruff. "The one who did this?" There was anger in his voice, and he touched her chin where the scar ended.

"No." She pulled back and stood up. "I didn't know him very well. He was with one other."

"Indian?" Miig asked.

She nodded, and Rose squeezed my hand a little. We were always excited at the possibility of more of us. Miig must have seen the looks on our faces, the sudden excitement, because he said, "Not every Indian is an Indian."

We stayed there in silence until the fire died out, then made our way to the tents.

THE FOUR WINDS

WE HEADED NORTHWEST, up towards the shallows of James Bay where the whales used to migrate before they packed up and headed down to Australia for good.

After the Indians left, the industries and businesses in and around their territories closed up too: small-time fisheries, hunting camps, tourist traps. After that, the big ones started to fall: large-scale resorts, fly-in luxury cottages, and wilderness getaways for stressed businessmen and their foreign investors. In light of the wars and the rush to adapt and survive, no one really gave a shit about tourism, gross domestic profit, or low-level jobs for rurally located folks. Though they cared enough to kick everyone out when the former employees tried to bunk down in the once-plush rooms and make use of the supplies and heat. They fenced them off, boarded them up, and some even hired security firms to walk around the perimeter and make sure no one was looking to survive on corporate-sponsored vacancy.

This is where we were now, up against the high fences surrounding Four Winds Resort, according to the faux-marble sign at the end of the weed-cracked driveway on the other side.

"Ten, maybe twelve feet." Chi-Boy was eyeing the top of the fence. "Razor wire edging. Electric charge mechanism."

"I doubt they're still electrified. That would mean the generators still worked." Miig sounded more hopeful than he looked. "Only one way to find out, I suppose."

Miig put his packsack on the ground, pulled the sash off his forehead, and let his bedroll drop behind his feet. He spit into his palms and rubbed them together.

"Okay." He took a deep breath and squared his shoulders.

I saw what he meant to do when he nudged his bedroll out of the way and took a few steps back, shaking out his arms and rolling his head on the stem of his neck.

"Shiiiiit ..." Rose hissed like a recoiling snake, her hand reaching to cover RiRi's eyes in anticipation of Miig dancing an electric jig, sizzling like a piece of frying meat.

I saw it in Chi-Boy's face, the way he suddenly looked young; I saw it in Minerva's eyes before they snapped shut behind wrinkles clenched like fat fists; I felt it in my own pulse — Miig was too important to lose. We couldn't manage without him, and yet here he was, about to take a run at a potentially electrified fence so that we could be sheltered and fed for another night.

I locked my eyes on Rose, on that bowed cord of vein and muscles that curved from her earlobe down her neck to her collarbone, and took a quick step to the right and forward. Before Miig could start his run, before I could lose my nerve, I reached out and took two chain links in my fingers.

I felt the electricity enter my hand, shoot up my arm, and land like a ball of hornets in my aorta. I swear I did. But it was just adrenaline, because there were no sparks, no smell of

barbecue pork, no blindness. There was just that stream of
breath and blood and tension rolling from Rose's ear down under
the collar of her faded parka.

"We're good." I wanted it to sound more confident, bigger,
with more nonchalant swagger. Instead it sounded like the squeak
of a sixteen-year-old boy who had to check with the back of his
left hand that he hadn't just wet himself.

I released the links and pushed my shaking hand through
my hair to give it somewhere to hide. Chi-Boy slapped me on the
shoulder before he leapt onto the fence with a Pendleton blanket
thrown across the back of his neck like a towel. He clambered to
the top. Minerva clapped and smiled, watching him go like a tall
Cree monkey, the stress smoothed away from her opened eyes.

Chi-Boy tossed the Pendleton over the razor wire at the top
and scrambled over. He walked his way down about eight feet
and then dropped the rest of the way with just the smothered
crunch of gravel to mark his arrival. Wab herded the group over
to the huge front gates. They waited there as Chi-Boy carefully
snapped the glass window in the guard booth and slid it out of
its frame. He slipped his long body through the square hole to
search out a key or some kind of mechanism that would allow
the others in without having to climb.

"No one is more important than anyone else, French."

It was Miig, still standing a few steps back. "No one should be
sacrificed for anyone else."

I tried to laugh it off, shrugging and starting a stream of "no
big deal" sentiments, but he refused to allow it.

"I'm not joking, boy." He held my gaze until the smile disappeared from my face and my cheeks began to burn. Only then
did he bend to gather up his things and walk over to the rest of

the group by the front gates. If they had heard, no one let on.

I was busy feeling sorry for my unappreciated heroics and myself in general and didn't see Rose there until she briefly took my hand. There was that electricity again, except this time the hornets had bilious wings because they swarmed, with texture and speed, from my heart down to my groin.

She pressed the pad of her thumb into the shaking center of my hand, then let it go and walked away. That was all. The smile returned, slightly, in the wake of Miig's reproach.

The gates popped open with a metallic screech and we slipped through the small gap rust and atrophy would allow. Chi-Boy waited for me to step through last and then locked the gates back up by hand, then he slid by me in the shadows and made his way to the front, but off to the side so he could scout. I finally looked up when we turned the bend in the driveway and caught my breath.

I'd spent most of my early life in the crumbling east end of the city, surrounded by urban decay and concrete waste where the skyline looked like a ruined mouth of rotted teeth. That is, except for these last few years out in the bush where we ran and home was a campfire and a canvas tent, not that it was bad. It's just that neither extreme had prepared me for the Four Winds Resort.

From the outside it looked like an oversized cottage, all wood and peaks and log pillars holding up odd angles and juts. It rose three storeys with a front entranceway that stretched out the front as a long corridor. We made our way to the doors and waited while Chi-Boy snapped the locks off with the cutters he kept in his roll. Then Tree and Zheegwon pried off the boards and opened the old doors with much effort and squealing of joints. Miig watched the darkness beyond the gates nervously.

The moon lit the wide front hall in pale ribbons, turning the dust and broken bits of chair and wainscoting and climbing vines from feral houseplants into fairy tale turrets. We walked slowly, out of habit, out of fear, but also, now, out of reverence. This space felt untouched. We could feel the thrum of old activity sliding along the floorboards, caught in the keyholes of closed doors. Everything had been shut tight while so much was still supposed to happen. The intent and plans hadn't had time to vacate. And here we were now opening the lid of a sealed jar, and all the anticipation of a tomorrow planned a thousand yesterdays ago came skittering to our feet like slick-shelled beetles.

The lower windows were all boarded up on either side of the hallway, done professionally with sheets of reinforced plywood, backed with crossed two-by-fours. But the skylight arching out over the hallway above showed us the night through glass opaque with greasy animal prints, bird shit, and weather. Still, there were stars, and we passed down the hall two by two, like visiting dignitaries underneath them.

At the end of the hallway was a dark hole. The glass ceiling and boarded-up walls ended, and whatever lay ahead was covered in silence and blackness. We gathered at the dark opening, waiting to know what to do.

Once our eyes adjusted we could make out lighter rectangles of grey on the far extremes of the space. That's where Miig and Chi-Boy went, to the lighter patches in the unknown. I kept my eyes to the right and saw Miig's hands suddenly dark on the grey. He pulled back what I understood then to be drapes, and swatches of sky diluted the dark with soft moonlight. He passed by a stone mantle set in the wall and repeated the same on the other side.

Across the room Chi-Boy also found floor-length windows on either side of a stone-mantled fireplace.

We took in the room, quickly at first to scan for danger, and then with more care to see everything we could in this space that was not forest or dilapidated barn.

"Do you think the fireplaces still work?" Wab was almost happy, which was a strange tone coming from her serious face.

Miig shook his head. "Doesn't matter. We can't use them. Fire comes with smoke, and this isn't a low campfire. Those chimneys would push smoke up past the tree line pretty damn quick."

The curves of her shoulders slumped, but she said nothing in return.

"But we can light up all these candles here." He touched a cream-colored pillar nearly the circumference of RiRi on the mantle. There were more alongside it of various heights and widths. There were even more on the low, round table in front of the fireplace.

"What're these?" It was Slopper. He ran his hands along a sheet-covered lump. There were two of them, one on either side of the table.

"Here." Chi-Boy yanked the edge of the sheet and a long, sage-hued sofa appeared. Slopper looked skeptical until Chi-Boy sat on it, tested the springs by bouncing a bit, and then lay down with an exaggerated sigh, folding his hands behind his head. Slopper ran around the table and pulled the sheet off the second one, getting tangled pretty good in voluminous folds and coughing from dust. With RiRi's help he was freed, and the pair bounced and giggled on the sofa's matched set.

Miig and Wab were lighting the candles and the room became lighter and smaller, the space more defined. After so much time in the wide-open, I was pleased to be contained. I sat on the edge of a couch and watched this new place illuminate.

The walls were cedar and the floors covered with carpet in a pattern of autumn leaves caught in a circular wind. Behind us, to the left of the entrance from the glass hallway, was a counter. There was an open space behind it and a wooden plaque hanging on the back wall with letters burned in: "Front Desk."

I walked over and around the counter and slid in behind. There was a telephone on the wall, the old kind with the curly cord attached. I picked it up, and its weight shocked me. I couldn't put it to my ear, the motion too foreign, so I placed it gently back in its metal cradle.

A stack of impossibly thick yellow books, the edges curling up like fiddleheads, were piled on the floor, leaning up against the wall. I crouched behind the counter and inspected a half wall of cubbyholes. In one was a shallow box of pens monogrammed with the same logo we'd seen on the sign outside the building. In another was a collection of little clips and fasteners of various sizes. In a half dozen others were papers, some written on, others sealed, some with line after line of careful script crossed out with thick colored lines. In a bottom hole was a six-pack of bottled water. I grabbed that and slid it above me, onto the counter.

"Woohoo, water!" I heard stomping as RiRi and Slopper bounded over to retrieve the precious find. Then the reproach of the others, warning them not to open it yet, to wait, to ration. I laughed to myself imagining Slopper's cheeks hanging in disappointment.

Beside the cubbies was a very long, very narrow drawer, as tall as the counter it was set into and only wide enough to accommodate a coin-sized handle.

"What's this?" I gave it a good yank, anticipating the resistance of time and atrophy so that when it slid easily open, I fell on my ass, knob still in hand. There was the clatter of metal on metal.

Miig came forward, bending on a knee. "Keys." He read the numbered plates, then looked up to the stairs curving up to a second floor from either side of the great room. "Room keys."

We shuffled up the stairs, kicking balls of dust and busted plaster as we went. As was custom, Miig and Chi-Boy took up the vulnerable front and back positions. Everyone but Minerva held a candle. I stood as tall as I could behind Miig, peering over his shoulder ahead and down over the railing into the great room lit on the far side by the remaining candles. I tried to open my eyes as far as I could to be as useful as possible. I was focused, but not so much so that I couldn't feel Rose reaching for my elbow when we got to the top.

Wab carried the keys in the cradle she'd made out of the front her sweater and they slid against each other like low metallic groans. We turned towards the dark in front and illuminated a flickering tunnel of doors. Each one was labeled with a small plaque inscribed with a number. Wab walked the line and handed a key to each person. Miig nodded, and Chi-Boy went to the first door on the right side of the hall with the matched key. He put it into the lock, filled his lungs with air so his shoulders rose halfway to his ears, and pushed.

The suck of air was audible and popped low in my eardrum like a lid being lifted. And when Chi-Boy disappeared into the room, I panicked a bit and crossed the hall to take up the space he'd left in the doorway. Chi-Boy walked the perimeter of the room before setting the candle down on a small round table in front of another empty fireplace, on a much smaller scale than those in the great room. He moved to the bed set against the wall and slowly folded his length on top of the comforter. It was big enough to for six pillows, side by side and stacked three deep. He adjusted the pillows under his head and nuzzled into the skin of the made bed like a child. It made me smile, seeing Chi-Boy, the fierce scout, bending his arms under his head, wiggling his ass to get into the softness with a goofy grin on his face.

I ran back out to the hallway and down to the door with my number on it. The lock was stiff and I turned it twice before it gave and the door swung in. RiRi was behind me, holding her candle at my elbow. I could feel the pinch of its heat. She gasped into the space — a whole empty, contained space — and followed me in. I threw open the curtains covering the windows on the far wall and illuminated the carpet on the floor. It was a mass of vines and blooms that twisted sinisterly in the flame but sat, docile and domestic, in the moonlight.

"This place is huge," she said.

"I know."

"Who needs this much space?" she asked.

"Not sure." I pulled off my torn boots with the toe of the other stepping on the heel. It felt wrong to tromp around in outside shoes.

"You didn't check for snakes first, Frenchie!" She was upset.

"Sorry, Ri." I took the candle from her and walked the perimeter of the room, holding it under the small table and dropping to my knees to check under the bed. The corners were choked with dust and it smelled like a whole metropolis of mice had lived and bred there, probably until the cats got wise and moved in before moving on, but no snakes.

"All clear. No snakes. Just some regular old monsters under the bed, that's it."

"Really?" Rose answered from just inside the door. "I knew we shoulda stopped to grab holy water for the buggers on the way in here."

I smiled. I couldn't help the size of it, either. She made me look stupid when she was around.

"C'mon, Rose, let's go into your room next." RiRi grabbed her by her forearm and spun her out of the room, making Rose's long dark hair fan out and settle across her shoulders like a shawl.

We each checked into a room, made ourselves comfortable, and then trudged back down the stairs to grab our gear and bring up the other candles. There was no use risking theft or discovery because of a few pinpoints of light reflected in an abandoned window. It was strange, all of us separated by walls, divided into compartments like bees in a dusty hive, so we kept our doors open. I could hear RiRi laughing and the rhythmic thump of bedsprings as someone jumped. She and Slopper ran up and down the hall a few times before Slopper, wheezing and holding his rounded side, huffed, "All right, enough, jeez. Let's lay down a bit."

Miig paced the hall every hour, always on patrol, and Wab spent a long time in Minerva's room getting her washed up and ready for bed. Minerva was beside herself with joy. She would have spent the longest in a real bedroom before the hunt began, way more than any of us. I heard her speak in full, lovely sentences from my room across the hall.

"Where's my nightie?" she asked.

"You don't have a nightie, Minerva. But look, you can change into your summer dress to sleep in tonight."

"I need to boil some tea, there. We should have some tea."

"We can't have a fire tonight, Min. How about let's split one of these waters before bed."

"Make sure you close the curtains again, you. If you sleep in that moonlight you'll wake up blind."

"Okay. There, they're all shut."

"No, no. Don't put out those candles yet. Bring the girls in. I wanna tell yous about the rogarou tonight."

I caught my breath. An old-timey story! I heard Wab come to the hallway and whistle a two-note tune, then RiRi and Rose shuffled in. I stayed in my room until they were settled, then crept into the hall and settled by the open door. The rise and fall of Slopper's soft snore spilled into the space. Tree and Zheegwon had filed into a single room and their door was closed, locking them in together. And there was no flickering coming from either Miig's or Chi-Boy's rooms, which meant they were either asleep or on patrol, so I was safe from discovery.

"This is my grand-mère's story, told to me when me and my sisters were turning into women. It's about Rogarou, the dog that haunts the half-breeds but keeps the girls from going on the roads at night where the men travel.

"'Down by the river to draw water, I feel eyes on the back of my neck, smell the blood on his tongue even with sweetgrass tight under my arm. I stand and turn fast, already drawing spit against the back of my teeth, hissing like a badger. But no, the Rogarou just watches. Didn't even blink, him.

"'Yes, Rogarou. I know one when I see it. Too big to be a dog, black as pitch, eyes yellow as new ragweed. I try to ignore him; turn my back even. But still, I hear him breathing. Not panting like a real dog, just slow ins and outs like a calm, everyday man. So I turn again, this time raising my arms to make me bigger. My sweetgrass fall all around my feet, I remember. I can smell it real strong, even over his stench. I growl, a throat sound with no gut in it. He looks up at my hands, and then stands up all smooth like smoke in the coldest sky. All air, no wind.

"'Yes, now I am intimidated, but no fear. There is no time for that nonsense. He is bigger than old Pitou Magnon, and that man was a giant amongst Christians. What happen next is my old trapline instincts. I still hold that heavy dipper for da water; it is still in my hand, and I bring it across the space between us; now I see him, he's moved to right here, in front of me. That old dipper, my mother carved that from the birch we stripped out back and gave it to me when Pierre died. She said it was heavy enough to chase off hungry men. But a widow in this settlement has no need. Up till now, it has only been used for water. Till now, when it became the Rogarou beating stick.

"'That dipper lands straight on the tender of the beast's nose. Oh mon Dieu! The noise, the terrible "crack" like a buffalo gun. Then nothing. I see the thing looking straight at me, and then a gash opens up all slow and oozing on the top of its snout. And as the good Lord is my witness, when that first drop of blood lands on its thick chest, he changes. More terrible cracks and tears.

"'I watch bones moving under his skin, the fur comes off in clumps. And all the while his insides are moving his outsides like fish spawning in the shallows. Oh, it is sickening; reminds me of lying in childbed. At the end of it, his limbs are too long, but human, and there he stands, a tall, naked man. And he has that hunger there, I see it same way I sees it in the men sometimes.'"

"Okay, Minerva, it's getting late." Wab, sensing a dark turn in the tale, tried to cut her off. "I need to get RiRi into bed now."

"Awww, Wab. I wanna hear the story about the dog some

more!" RiRi sounded tired, even through her protest. I heard feet hit the ground as she was made to stand from the bed and marched out the door.

I crouched to the side as they passed. After a minute, Minerva picked up the tale again, speaking in the heavily accented voice of her grandmother.

"'It starts with that violence and ends with that singing in my guts — another kind of violence. He comes as beast and I make him bleed. It started with that dipper, then it was a switch cut from that same birch, then I grew tired of tools. As we become more like man and wife, year after year, I bite him the way I thought he would like to bite me. When I bring the blood, he brings the man. And mother and grand-mère and Catholic are all erased and I am just a woman.

"'I'm marked. Talk to the old man there, down at the shore. And he talks about Rogarous. I don't ask, I think he can just tell. He says they kill, unless met without fear. He says once you are marked, that dog will keep coming back. He says, even when you are on your deathbed, he will come. Every full moon, every year until you're in the ground. Then he looks for the next one, says he finds it in the family, and marks them the same way. Now I know I am damned, because my sin is my family's sin. Oh mon Dieu, who in this family deserves such a curse! Who in my own bloodline will have to miss the Jesus in the heavens because of my weakness?'"

There was a pause.

"Minerva?" Rose spoke softly.

Another space.

"Minerva?"

She was answered by a peal of crunchy snoring.

"Good night, Kokum."

I didn't have time to move back to my room before Rose was at the door, the candle she carried throwing my crouching shadow and her standing shadow into knots on the floor. I was embarrassed at being caught eavesdropping. She just gave me a small, tight smile and, with a weird look in her eye, turned away and disappeared into a doorway two up from this one. I slunk back to my room.

I slept in just my shorts, wrapped up under the stiff blankets, surrounded by a barrier of dense pillows. I let my candle stay lit. I knew it was an extravagance I would regret later when we didn't have any more portable light, but I enjoyed the way it flickered and jumped in the small breezes from the crumbling window panes, jumping against the walls and ceiling so that I remembered there were walls and ceilings around me once more.

Despite the long day and the late hour, I couldn't sleep. Slopper's and Minerva's snoring filled the hallway with familiarity and every now and then I heard a cough or a sneeze that reminded me we were all still together. Still, I could not sleep. Instead, I stared at the small shadows and big emptiness of the starless ceiling.

There was a creak and a click and my door was shut. I pulled myself up quick onto my elbows, eyes adjusting to reach into the dark. When she got almost to the other side of the wide bed and into the circle of the candle's glow, I saw that it was Rose, and I stopped breathing.

She was wearing a grey T-shirt that fell midway down her lean thighs. Her braid was undone and her hair hung in black waves. She looked directly at me, but didn't smile. There was something else on her face, though. My breathing came back in double time. My heart was an echo in my ears.

She climbed onto the bed, and I moved over a bit to give her space. Still looking at me, she lifted the covers and slid under, beside me. I felt the complete length of her then like a warm sliver under my ribs. It was the best thing I'd ever felt. It made me brave, and I adjusted my arm so that it was a pillow under her head, so that all that soft hair could cover it like a web.

Then she began talking.

"Everyone in my family is short, every last one of us. When I was younger and we still had the house, my mother would pull out old photos of her people. Not the printed-up kind from computers, but the shiny kind on real film papers. Every one of her relatives was tiny, even when they were fat their height made them compact. My mom barely cleared five feet. My dad, well, he came from a less challenged lineage. He was from the islands, and his people were pretty damn tall. He stood around five foot ten. Me, I was eight pounds when I was born, and my mother never forgave me for it.

"My mom said her family came from the White River reserve before it was amalgamated into the wider Kenora band and then moved. She met my dad there when they brought over the last few families from Grassy Narrows. He was a student from the University of Winnipeg, studying our plants and their medicines. My parents were taken together, right at the beginning of the experiments before people knew they had to run like the devil himself was pissing on their heels. They didn't care he was half black and his kind of Indian was the kind from the warm oceans. Guess they were less picky when it came to brown. I was only five when they left me with my granny. We played a lot of euchre.

"She sent me out with my great-uncles when they decided to hit the bush. She was too slow, she said, to come with us. So we left her in her little house on the old reserve lands she refused to leave, with a dozen jugs of clean water and a pantry half full of cans. She said that was plenty, that any more would be wasted.

"I walked into the bush with my granny's brothers, William and Jonas, one afternoon and kept walking for six years before the first one fell ill. We set up camp when he couldn't go on. We stayed there a full year before Will passed. We even grew a little patch of corn with seeds we'd brought from down south. After we buried him, Jonas and I packed up and started the walk again. We ran into a person every now and then, but Jonas never wanted to stay with them or have anyone come with us. He said he was charged with protecting me and he couldn't trust no one with a little girl around. Jonas said our family had survived residential schools back in the old times and those stories were kept on down the line. He wouldn't tell me much — he barely spoke now that Will was in the ground — but he did tell me to trust no one and to always make sure the camp was clear before I bedded down at night.

"'A child needs walls. Not brick and wood walls all the time, but some sort of walls to keep them in and others out. So they can play and they can sleep and they can move without the burden of eyes and hands. I'm that wall for you. When I'm gone, you make your own walls with this,' Jonas told me, and he held out Will's hunting rifle to me. I learned to hunt small with wires, and bigger with that gun. Jonas and I, we walked for hours and days and months together. We didn't really talk. He showed me things, though.

"'You're a woman now,' he told me a few years ago, right after I turned thirteen. 'That's what you follow now.' He pointed to the full, silver moon with two bent fingers. 'That's your granny.'

"About eight months ago, Jonas didn't wake up.

"I dug the hole while he was still breathing. Because I wasn't sure if I'd have the guts to do anything once he was gone. Once I was just me.

"Thought about turning around, heading back to my granny, but I knew there was no turning around. I could see as sure as a fire in the trees that they were there and she wasn't. That she'd been swallowed up, though my bets were on her taking herself out before the schools could.

"I stayed by Jonas's grave for four days and four nights. On the last night the full, silver moon hung low in the sky like a heavy rock in a plastic bag, ready to tear through the bottom onto your toes. Then I knew it was time. I cleaned up. I packed up. And I walked. And now, well, here I am."

When she was done, she settled her chin in the crook of my collarbone. Her breath poured into the space like tea into a cup. I felt the brush of her bottom lip on my skin there and the small hairs on my arms lifted. She squeezed in closer, her stomach making contact with my side, bringing my full body to attention. I moved my free hand over the front of my shorts.

"'Shit." I tried pushing it away. I swallowed hard and breathed slow and steady, like you do when you have game in sight and you don't want to scare it off. I hoped the concentration would take my excitement away. But then she moved her hand to cover mine and I almost died. It was such exquisite clarity of blood and skin and breath that I felt like crying. Instead I let her lace her fingers through mine and tilted my neck so that my face lined up with hers.

Her eyes were half closed, lips open. She was the most beautiful girl in the world and we were in a bed together. I watched the candlelight make red stars in her irises and thanked the Jesus

I'd left it on. She moved her face forward, just a few centimeters, and I took her lip between mine. She slid a knee over my thighs and pressed closer. My pulse was a hand drum in the cradle of my gut. I wasn't sure how long I could stand this before I just died from it. She pressed down on the front of my shorts with both our hands, and I couldn't have seen straight if my eyes had been open.

"French, can I sleep with you guys?"

We jumped, neither of us having heard the door open. RiRi stood at the foot of the bed, rubbing her eyes with a fist.

"Holy shit, Ri!" I sat bolt up, throwing Rose off to the side. "Holy hell, I didn't hear you come in."

She just stood there. I guess with no precedent to go by, she wouldn't really understand the concept of knocking. I sighed. It was Rose who threw back the covers and invited her in, pushing me further to the edge of the bed with a hip. "Come here, babe. Get in. It's cold out there."

She scrambled up the bed and jumped in beside Rose, pulling the older girl's arm over her like a comforter. I tried to curl myself around Rose's back, but the intimacy was further broken by RiRi's feet thrown backwards over Rose's knees so that they jabbed into my legs like rounded icicles. Still, I was making the best of it, enjoying the smell of Rose's hair across the pillow, pushing my sore groin into her backside a bit, when Slopper appeared behind me.

"Move over, French. I can't sleep."

"Christ, what's wrong with everyone. I heard you snoring a minute ago."

He just shrugged his heavy shoulders and pushed his way in behind me. And that was that.

I WOKE UP when Minerva started coughing. The sound was deafening as she was sitting in one of the tufted chairs in front of the fireplace in my room. I jumped when I saw her there. How long had she been sitting in my room? She waved to me when I lifted my head. I tried to wave back, but I couldn't lift my arm. In fact, my head was the only thing I could move. Slopper drooled on the pillow beside me and Rose was stretched out, her head back on my arm, on the other side. Beside her was RiRi, arms thrown out wide like she was making a great leap in her dreams. Our feet were trapped under a weight on top of the blankets that turned out to be Tree and Zheegwon lying perpendicular on top of the comforter.

I slid my arm out from under Rose, an almost painful separation, and climbed over Slopper, almost stepping on Chi-Boy, who was stretched out beside the bed, a discarded pillow under his head. Beside him was Wab. There were a few inches between them, but their breathing was matched, an even greater intimacy than touch.

So we were all here, crammed into one room, all of us besides Miig.

"Morning, French. I see we ended up having a slumber party last night."

Spoke too soon. There he was, stretching out his arms above his head while he leaned up against the wall to the right of the closed door, his legs crossed in front of him.

I gave him a half smile and combed my hair with my fingers, smoothing it back and down, sitting on the edge of my full bed.

How the hell did everyone end up in here? I tried to remember. The memory of Rose punched me in the gut, and I stepped over Chi-Boy and Wab to the adjoining bathroom to empty my bladder and catch my breath. Of course, there was no running water, so I pissed down the sink and examined my face in the foggy mirror above it.

AT THE END of day two at the Four Winds, Miig was already getting antsy. Everything in his gut sang "move, move, move." And Miig was a man who lived by his gut. I could see Chi-Boy already scouting the property for things to take with us. In the corner of the great room he'd stacked a wool blanket with wide colored stripes, a couple of knives out of the kitchen block, a dozen candles, a box of matchbooks stamped with the resort logo, every piece of food left in the pantry, which amounted to maybe twenty-five cans of beans and six cans of powdered milk, and a stainless steel kettle. What he didn't stack there, but what I saw him slip into his bedroll when I was supposed to be checking behind the desk for maps of the area (which I found on the back of a placemat) was a lady's trapper's hat made from white fur with a thin leather ribbon tie dangling from the flaps. He'd found it in one of the storage rooms in the back and secreted it out to his bags under the folds of his grey sweater. I pretended to not notice.

Outside, Miig had found a shed, and though it was pretty well scavenged from when they first shut up shop, he did manage to find a two-wheeled cart, the kind you tow behind a four-wheeler.

"We'll patch up these tires and take it with us. It might prove to be more burden than asset, so we'll test it out for a few days. If it works, it'll do for hauling Minerva on her off days." He took Tree and Zheegwon with him to try to repair the tires and test its weight capacity.

Right now Minerva had found a rocking chair on the back porch of the building. There was a whole row of them out there, facing the back wall where thick sheets of wood had been nailed up against what must have been huge picture windows facing some kind of million-dollar view.

I was on patrol and wandered the building, hoping to find some new thing that would make Miig agree to stay. Here we had beds and warmth and walls. It was luxurious. I didn't want to leave. And if I were being completely honest I'd admit it had more to do with Rose's visit to my bed last night than anything else, a phenomenon that could maybe be coaxed out of heaven a second time. But I wasn't admitting anything.

I followed a side hallway off the main room into the nest of tiny offices that lay back there — a janitor's supply closet, a long room with lockers on either side, some still locked, others open with photographs taped to the inside and work jackets hung up, and finally a room with a desk and mountains of paper with a plaque reading "Manager" on the door. I found Wab sitting behind the desk in the manager's office with a bottle balanced on a pile of yellowed printouts in front of her. When she lifted her head, she looked sleepy with her eyes half closed and a straight grimace on her lips.

"Hey, Wab."

She took a couple of deep breaths. I waited, shifting my weight from one foot to the other, fixed in her stare. "Do you know how shitty my mom was?" she asked me.

I stared down at the tops of my taped-up boots. How should I answer?

"So shitty, dude. So, so, super shitty."

This was the most she'd ever said directly to me. It was terrifying.

"You have a shitty mom, Frenchie?" She picked up the bottle and spun the cap with the side of her hand. It came off the bottle and flew across the desk, clattering to the floor like a plastic coin.

I shook my head. "No."

"Good for you, man. Good for you." She took a short swallow from the bottle and put it down hard.

"You know what I did before I got here?"

I looked up at her. She wasn't looking at me anymore. She was tipping the bottle side to side, watching the amber liquid slosh and wave.

"No."

"I ran." She laughed with no joy, like a cough racked with sickness.

I backed away from the door. I felt like she should be alone, not sure I wanted her to keep talking.

Instead, she got dark, stood as on a wire, and made her way around the desk. I didn't move, not sure of what my role was here, or if she even still saw me. I wasn't sure until she fell on my neck and sobbed, right as Chi-Boy came around the corner.

Wab was the one I was the most anxious around until Rose joined the group. We were all a little uneasy around her, I think. She was hard to figure out. Harder even than Miig or Minerva; their personas were clear. Their trauma was stark and motivating. Wab's was less defined, messier somehow, and therefore more dangerous.

Wab was movie star beautiful, all tall and harsh. When I first came to the group, she was still wearing an eye patch, like a real villain. Now she just faced the world with one eye, a long red slash from her right cheekbone to the middle of her forehead over the other. The scar had knotted itself into raw seam that closed the socket forever.

Her teeth were straight and white. Her hair was down to her

butt and burnt a warm umber from the sun. She chopped wood
better than Miig and was stingy with her words. She could crush
aluminum cans with a bent flex of calf and thigh, and every boy,
myself included for as long as I could remember, had at one point
or another harbored a secret crush and more than a few nighttime fantasies over Wab.

We'd begged Miig for her coming-to story, since she'd never
waste enough words to share it herself. We'd been on a hunt the
last time we really drilled him for info on our mysterious love
interest, a little before Rose showed up.

"I heard, after she killed a man with a pair of scissors in the
city, that she pulled her own eye out so she'd never have to look
at herself in the mirror again," Slopper had said with round eyes
and dramatic breaths.

"I heard she was a mercenary for one of the West Side gangs,"
said Tree.

"And that she lost her eye when an East Side gang attacked their
clubhouse," said Zheegwon.

"And that when she woke up and saw her eye was missing, she
found the East Siders," said Tree.

"And killed them all, removing the right eye from each body
before she left for the bush," finished Zheegwon.

Chi-Boy just laughed at us. Miig leaned over the trap he was
trying to show us how to reset and beckoned us in with a lowered
voice. "Then I guess you boys better be careful who you dream
about without her pants on." We turned four shades of red;
even Chi-Boy was a little pink in the neck, revealing that maybe
his dreams were a little more than wolves and Grandfather
Teachings.

"Besides," he'd added as went back to hooking the spring in its latch, "everyone tells their own coming-to story. That's the rule. Everyone's creation story is their own."

Together, Chi-Boy and I carried her to the main room and set her on the couch, still teary, but silent again. The twins ran and got Miig, who lit a small smudge for Wab. Normally we'd bring everyone together for a smudge, but the air was dark and the littlest kids were safe on the back porch in rocking chairs with Minerva.

Wab took handfuls of thick smoke and rubbed her face. I wasn't sure she'd talk. Miig sat quietly beside her, staring at his fingers laced into each other. Rose and I sat cross-legged on the floor beside the table. Chi-Boy hovered nearby, uncomfortable with uselessness. The twins leaned on each other on the opposite couch.

Then she began.

WAB'S COMING-TO STORY

BEFORE THEY EMPTIED out, the inner cities were swarming with desperation-hungry bellies, pinched guts, lousy scalps, dirty necks, and the people who made money off of it all. The alleys grew lean-tos and shelters made of layers of melting cardboard like hives. The apartments were stuffed to overflowing, and people huddled in the hallways. They made their homes in the stairwells after every room was taken, so that once the elevators were shut off you had to bribe your way through living rooms and sleeping babies to get to and from your apartment.

I lived on the top floor with my mother. She drank. Men came. Men left. One day my older brother Niibin stopped coming home and it was just the two of us — the two of us and the revolving parade of men with dirt-stiff jeans and bloodied knuckles. Sometimes they came after me, waking me up from my sleep when they tried to jam their rough hands in my pajamas. Sometimes they got more than just a feel before I could fend them off and lock myself in the bathroom. I hated it there. There were more bugs than food in the kitchen. And when they shut off the water first and then the power next, it stunk and the rats came, braver than the bugs, more invasive then the men. Eventually, after the raids started, someone set fire to the building trying to cook Spam over a hall fire and me and mom were on the street.

I was ten then, and I watched the military shuttling the cleaner citizens to new settlements and gated communities. We hid in a Dumpster we shared with a mute named Freddie when the school staff came for the Indians. Freddie was Malaysian, but he wasn't taking any chances. Freddie's wife had been carried away at the food bank and she was from Taiwan, but no one believed her. There was good money in snitching on Indians, and people would call in if a Swedish girl wore a braid in her hair. That's why we stopped going to the food banks: the volunteers called in Indian sightings and next thing you knew, a wave of white vans screeched up and off you went, kicking and screaming, watching yourself in the mirrored reflection of their sunglasses, throwing boxes of macaroni and cheese and screaming to some god or devil or anything in between. We'd heard too many stories about the death camps, the way we were being murdered real slow.

One time, we were half a block away when they showed up. We watched them carry off an old man and his grandson before we remembered to run. I'll never forget the way that man looked when they tossed his grandson in the back of the van like a bag of rice. I watched his soul fold up on itself like a closing door. The light and warmth and humanity clapped shut in his eyes because he couldn't protect the one thing that mattered. There was no coming back from that, even if he did manage to walk away later on, which he wouldn't.

My mom traded favors for booze since food wasn't really her priority. She might have already known she was dying by then, anyway. I wonder if you can feel poison in your blood? If your veins feel tighter or your pulse gets thicker somehow? Anyway, I was left to feed myself.

I was a runner and I could go for hours without having to stop or even slow down. The way a good sprint turns your breath to a low whistle, the way it spring-loads your knees: that was my drink. I was addicted. At first I'd run for the joy of it. But once we ran out of food, I did it in trade. You needed a message brought to your brother on the west side of the city after phone service was cut? I was your messenger. You needed medicine and weren't well enough to get to the pharmacist? I was your girl. But it wasn't free. You had to put gas in the car if you wanted it to drive. I charged a tin of soup for a short jaunt, a full loaf of bread and a jar of pasta sauce for trip any longer than the immediate neighborhood. And business was good. After the phones were cut, cell service was blocked in an effort to persuade the leftovers to either move into the new developments or to fuck off and die. It also made it easier to isolate the Indigenous and stunt the growth of community. I was in demand. And for something other than what was under my PJs.

I ran for a whole year before they caught me. Not the government assholes. Just regular assholes. Everyday assholes. The kind of assholes that move around in packs because they're too weak to be alone.

They caught me on a bogus run they'd put in, sending a stupid hillbilly-lookin' Indian hopped up on opiates to commission a run. I'd seen him around enough to nod when he passed me. Sometimes he was with my mother. And I recognized his state well enough not to slow down. Today, though, he came with a job.

"Easy money," he said, drooling onto the back of his hand.

"Nothing serious," he lied, handing over Danishes in advance as payment. I should have known right then.

I was to deliver a sealed envelope to the West Side by sundown. I ate two of the Danishes right off. They were good, not even two days stale. I put the remainder in my backpack. I should have eaten them all then and there. I should have never taken them to begin with.

I set off full speed, sucking sugar out of my molars and just real pleased with myself. I ran down the tracks left in the potholed road from the old streetcar line. When I got to the building in the west, there were two guys standing guard out front. They had baseball bats, real ones, not the whittled two-by-fours most people carried, and wore sunglasses. I should've never shown them the envelope. I should have thought better about following them inside the double front doors of the old deli when they started laughing.

Inside it was cold and mostly empty. There was another guy behind the old counter, wiping down the steel surfaces in the front kitchen and serving area. In the main room were a couple of round tables with broken chairs. There was another group of men there, quiet now as I walked past with my letter held in front of my chest, like it would keep me safe.

I followed the guard into the back, all eyes on me, where I found a man with red kinky hair and a wide nose sitting at a low desk.

"So," he said as he stood up, "you're the runner, yeah?"

I tried to stay hard. "Boy, you're a master of observation."

He threw his head back and laughed. His front teeth had been sharpened to points by bone or grinding or evolution, I couldn't be sure. My legs started to shake. He stood and walked around the desk, sitting on the edge of it directly in front of me, arms across his thick chest.

"She's feisty," he remarked to the guard on my left. "I like that." They chuckled together.

"Here's your letter. Paid in full. I'll be going now."

I extended the letter to him, pushing it against his nylon track suit jacket.

"Wait, wait now, runner. Don't you wanna see what's inside?"

"None of my business." I shrugged, still holding out the envelope he wasn't taking.

"Oh, you'll want to stay for this." He finally grabbed it, running a long, smooth finger along my hand when he did. The guards moved in tight on either side of me as the redhead took the envelope back to the desk and sat in his taped-up leather chair.

He tapped it on his forehead. "You see, runner, I have a new business venture I've been trying to get off the ground. I have this idea that we can provide services where the fair city of Toronto has decided to rescind theirs." He pointed with the envelope to the guards on either side of me and to the door. I turned to see the men from the front room gathered there. Watching. Waiting. The Danishes in my stomach turned to gas and burn.

"But." He tore open the end of the envelope and blew inside. "Seems like someone already beat us to it. Nobody wants to pay the prices we've set for our communications excellence on account of some squaw bitch who'll do it for a tin of food." He turned the envelope upside down and shook it. Nothing came out.

Decoy.

"Fuck."

I turned, tried to run, adrenaline kicking into my joints like electricity. The guards looped their big arms in mine and lifted me clean off the ground. The redhead laughed, and the group at the door, they joined in now, making their way into the room, eyes flashing. I kicked and swore and swung my trapped limbs so hard my braid wiped at my own eyes, so I closed them.

I didn't see when they carried me to the broken freezer, when they locked me in and lined up outside. I only saw for one minute when the redhead made his way in first, unzipping his jacket and untying his pants.

"Look at me."

I opened my eyes. He stood there in the freezer light, brown chest bare, a silver knife in his hand. "You're gonna stop your little business, yeah."

I nodded quick, all my bravado gone, breathing so hard my nose burned.

"I'm gonna make sure of it." He moved fast, too quickly for me to do anything but close my eyes again. I didn't feel the slice. Just the wet on my cheek, and neck, and chest. Then he was pulling off my pants. Then I stopped feeling all together.

Later, I heard I was there for two days. Two days in that freezer with the lineup replenishing itself every time it ended. And when they let me go, I limped out, holding my stomach, my eye already shriveled. I limped home to my Dumpster, to my mother, to Freddie the Malaysian. There was no more running. Instead, I hid. Freddie tried to clean me up and stitch my face, but it was already scarring. I didn't care. Neither did my mom. She'd started smoking crack, which was plentiful, to replace the booze, which was scarce. She barely moved out of the way of her own piss if she wasn't on the hunt for the next rock.

When I could walk, I did. One block, then another, then a field, past a line of trees, and into the bush.

Gone.

And the dick who set up the run, who handed over the Danishes and scurried off into the alleyways, that was the man I saw a week ago in the woods. I'm sure of it.

"IS HE COMING to take Wab back to the bad guys?

I jumped at the small voice behind me, pitched high with terror. RiRi had crept into the room.

"Did those bad guys work with the murderers? And why do they murder us slow?" She was on the verge of hysterics, trying to hold it back in the way she did when really scared.

God, how long had she been there? What did she hear? And how could I take it back?

"Oh God, no!" Wab was mortified, holding her hand over her mouth. She slumped down on the couch, shaking her head, eyes closed now.

Miig sighed and motioned RiRi forward.

"Come, daughter. Time to hear Story."

STORY: PART 2

THIS TIME MIIGWANS picked up where he'd left off the night that Rose first arrived.

"THE EARTH WAS broken. Too much taking for too damn long, so she finally broke. But she went out like a wild horse, bucking off as much as she could before lying down. A melting North meant the water levels rose and the weather changed. It changed to violence in some cases, building tsunamis, spinning tornados, crumbling earthquakes, and the shapes of countries were changed forever, whole coasts breaking off like crust.

"And all those pipelines in the ground? They snapped like icicles and spewed bile over forests, into lakes, drowning whole reserves and towns. So much laid to waste from the miscalculation of infallibility in the face of a planet's revolt.

"People died in the millions when that happened. The ones that were left had to migrate inward. It was like the second coming of the boats, so many sick people and not enough time to organize peacefully.

"But the powers that be still refused to change and bent the already stooped under the whips of a schedule made for a population twice its size and inflated by the need to rebuild. Those that were left worked longer, worked harder. And now the sun was gone for weeks at a time. The suburban structure of their lives had been upended. And so they got sicker, this time in the head. They stopped dreaming. And a man without dreams is just a meaty machine with a broken gauge.

"People lost their minds, killing themselves and others and, even worse for the new order, refusing to work at all. They needed answers, solutions. So, up here, the Governors turned to the Church and the scientists to find a cure for the missing dreams. In the meantime, those who could afford it turned to sleep counselors, took pills to go to bed and pills to wake up, and did things like group hypnosis to implant new dreams.

"At first, people turned to Indigenous people the way the New Agers had, all reverence and curiosity, looking for ways we could help guide them. They asked to come to ceremony. They humbled themselves when we refused. And then they changed on us, like the New Agers, looking for ways they could take what we had and administer it themselves. How could they best appropriate the uncanny ability we kept to dream? How could they make ceremony better, more efficient, more economical?

"That was the first alarm set off in the communities. We thought that was the worst of it. If only.

"We were moved off lands that were deemed 'necessary' to that government, same way they took reserve land during wartime. Because no one cared about long-range things like courting votes for the next election and instead cared about things like keeping valued, wealthy community members safe; there were no negotiations. We were just pushed off. The new migration from the coastlines was changing geography daily.

"And then, even after our way of life was being commoditized, after our lands were filled with water companies and wealthy corporate investors, we were still hopeful. Because we had each other. New communities started to form, and we were gathering strength. But then the Church and the scientists that were working day and night on the dream problem came up with their solution and everything went to hell.

"They asked for volunteers first. Put out ads asking for people with 'Indigenous bloodlines and good general health' to check in with local clinics for medical trials. They'd give you room and board for a week and a small honorarium to pay for your time off work. By then our distrust had grown stronger, and they didn't get many volunteers from the public. So they turned to the prisons. The prisons were always full of our people. Whether or not the prisoners went voluntarily, who knows? There weren't enough people worried about the well-being of prisoners to really make sure.

"It began as a rumor, that they had found a way to siphon the dreams right out of our bones, a rumor whispered every time one of us went missing, a rumor denounced every time their doctors sent us to hospitals and treatments centers never to return. They kept sending us away, enticing us to seek medical care and then keeping us locked up, figuring out ways to hone and perfect their 'solution' for sale.

"Soon, they needed too many bodies, and they turned to history to show them how to best keep us warehoused, how to best position the culling. That's when the new residential schools started growing up from the dirt like poisonous brick mushrooms.

"We go to the schools and they leach the dreams from where our ancestors hid them, in the honeycombs of slushy marrow buried in our bones. And us? Well, we join our ancestors, hoping we left enough dreams behind for the next generation to stumble across."

BACK INTO THE WOODS

THERE WAS SOMETHING beautiful about the way the woods were now. I had no context for a before and after comparison, but I knew that the way things were now could not have existed with so many people and so much scavenging before the wars and the relocations.

In this time, in this place, the world had gone mad with lush and green, throwing vines over old electrical poles and belching up rotten pipelines from the ground. Animals were making their way back, but they were different. Too much pollution and too much change. Miig said if we gave them another half a century, they'd take everything back over and we would be the hunted. But for now, like always, we couldn't sit around on the couches and contemplate our world and what might lie ahead. We were outside, getting ready.

Snow fell in a light dusting now. It looked like glitter scraped from the underside of clouds by the scrubby top branches of the pines. The skeletons of the green trees curved under the elegant weight of the snow, bowing and twisting like ribbons in the wind.

"Last snow of the season. Late, too. Damn seasons poke into one another with this new Earth." Miig put enough weight onto each of us so that we just began to buck, and then stopped, patting our loads and looking to the next one up to be burdened.

None of us were happy. We wanted to stay at the lodge. It was warm and had walls and made us feel less in danger, less chased. Maybe that's why he wanted us gone so quickly, before we lost the will and instinct to keep moving altogether.

Wab was still moving slower today after her binge, but if things had changed between us from her cracking wide open like that, she didn't let on. RiRi was quieter than usual, but she worked hard to process Story in silence, not wanting to prove our theories of her being too young to know the whole truth.

We pulled a load of heavy cans and propane canisters and a welded hibachi barbecue in the trailer cart we'd found out back of the resort, along with Minerva's share of the camp carry. For now she was doing okay. The few days inside had done her well, and she sang under her breath and into the top of her sweater, a nursery rhyme about a fiddle and a cat.

Had the few days at the Four Winds done me good, too? I wasn't sure. I'd gotten closer to Rose the first night, but then she'd fairly avoided me the rest of the time. I'd heard Wab's coming-to story, but I kind of wished I hadn't. It was still too torn on the edges to file away. Having to watch Ri's face from the truth of our predicament was gnawing on me, knowing that she knew there were no conversations to be had, no treaties left to be signed, that we were a product and that wasn't going to change any time soon. There was the run or there was death with nothing in between. And sleeping inside just made me dream about my brother. It was nice to see him, but always by the end of the dream he was gone, and in some horrible rending kind of way. Better to be in the forest, I thought. Where the dreams were shrouded in fog and cold and the group knew its order and stride by the weight of our want.

"We're into April now," Miig said. "See the buds on those trees?" He pointed up with his thin lips. "We'll have more cover soon. And more sickness because of the wet ground."

No time for sickness. At the beginning of winter most of us came down with a bad cough that shook our ribs and rattled our heads, which responded by leaking thick mucus into our scarves and onto our sleeves. Minerva boiled cedar branches and pine needles into medicine and fed it each of us every two hours.

"Sick makes her nervous," Zheegwon told me. "She lost a baby one year to the sick."

"Minerva had a baby?"

"No," responded Tree. "He was one of us, one of the leftovers. But he became hers and then one winter he died from cough."

I did see a panic in Minerva's eyes the next time she stopped to scoop thick medicine into us, opening her mouth to imitate what we should do, as if we were all sick babies she was trying to save. I'm not sure her old heart could take another round of sick and worry.

It was tough walking away from the resort. I looked back more than once. What if we had stayed there a bit longer? Would Rose have visited me in my bed again? Would she have gotten over whatever weirdness sat between us now and have even just fallen asleep on my shoulder by the candle fire? I'd never know for sure. I could dream about it, though. I was thankful for the gift of dreams more than ever.

Slopper and RiRi were still little so they were closer to the vicious edge than the rest of us. Their contempt for Miig and his power over the group seeped to the surface.

"Who made him Chief, anyway," Slopper moaned, kicking rocks as we started into the woods.

"Yeah, who?" echoed RiRi, kicking at the air beside her friend. Her anger was made cute with her little voice and slight lisp of youth. She was wearing a new pair of bright pink rubber boots. She'd found them under the bed in her room the first morning.

"Look! They're made outta candy," she'd said, then licked the shiny surface of one boot and cringed. "Not candy."

RiRi had never had candy, but she'd seen pictures and heard stories about it. So every time something was shiny or bright — and these boots were both — she assumed they were candy. It was a constant disappointing hunt for her.

"You goof." I laughed at her screwed-up face. "They're not candy, they're just shiny plastic. Put them on." I helped her out of her old runners that were too big and had been handed down from Slopper. The boots popped on, and she stood in them.

"They fit me, French!" she squealed, clomping down the hall one way and then back. I couldn't help but giggle along with her as she stomped by. When she got to the far end, though, she stopped, her little dark head hanging a bit.

"What's wrong? Do they pinch?"

"Maybe she was Nish. Maybe they took her outta her bed."

"What?"

She turned around. "Maybe the girl whose boots these are got taken. Maybe she had a bad dream and then they knew she was Nish and they called in the 'cruiters and they took her." There was a hitch between "took" and "her." She was close to tears.

"No way, RiRi. If she was Nish she would be too fast for any old Recruiter."

"No one would leave these." She looked down at her shiny feet. "No one would leave these on purpose." She couldn't believe her luck and assumed the worst for their backstory. Now that she knew what was really going on, her imagination had a dark streak in it.

"Nah." I tried to cheer her up. "I bet she was some rich kid, the kind with yellow curls and her very own pierced ears. I bet she just had so many shoes with her that she forgot this one pair. I bet she didn't even notice they were gone."

"Yeah." She stomped past me. "I'm going to find Slopper." She made her way down the stairs, jumping down one at a time.

I wasn't sure she'd bought my version of the origin of the boots, but the next day she was wearing them as she chased after Slopper through the huge front room with the double fireplaces.

We had been walking since daybreak. But it was noon before we smelled the smoke.

"Where's that coming from?" Slopper lifted his wide nose to the air like a puppy. "I smell cooking."

"No, that's not cooking, it's just smoke." I corrected.

"Why else would there be smoke?"

"Fire," replied Miig. He didn't seem shocked. He must have smelled it for the past mile, the old fox.

"Fire? Without cooking?" Slopper looked around for confirmation. "But why?"

"Haven't you ever heard of an accidental fire?" It was RiRi who answered. The fear in her face made me think she must have seen one of these accidental fires up close in her short lifetime. Or maybe it was more of that new dark streak.

Slopper mirrored her expression, though he shook his head no.

"French." Miig called me over to him. "I need you to climb that pine and check it out. Do a 360, wouldya?"

I nodded, wiggled out of my burden, and took a run at the tall tree he'd pointed out. I climbed hand over foot for as long as momentum would take me and then switched to a slower shimmy until the branches started and I could use them as steps. It grew quiet in the cushion of brush, the air thick with needles and sap. I paused for a minute and listened. My own breath, the measured thud of my heart, and the slow whoosh of a constant, cold wind. Despite the urgency, despite the world as it was at that moment, I felt content, maybe even a little more than that. I was alive and climbing a tree and a girl that I was weak for was safe on the ground below. And I was doing something strong to keep her safe, to keep all of them safe. I felt old-timey, and something lush burst open in my chest.

Then I resumed the climb, pulling myself from foothold to handhold until the branches thinned and the trunk narrowed so that my hands touched on the other side when I hugged it before the next shimmy up. I found a good crook to hold me steady and looked out.

The smoke coiled above the treetops, a single cumulous bloom of grey far enough to the west that it looked manageable. Below it the trees were moving in impossible directions, shaking back and forth, then swaying like fainting giants, then popping out of sight. Plumes of dust kicked up as they winked out. Straining, I heard the slow rumble of enterprise, a low, steady thrum. The disappearance of the trees paused and, when the dust settled to a solid haze, there was a flash of yellow in the gap. I sighed, not making sense of it, but understanding enough to know I had to get to Miig and relay the scene. I began the slow, controlled fall back down.

"Well, is it food?" Slopper called up through cupped hands when I was about ten feet up. Tree gave him a light chuck on the shoulder.

"What? A man can't be hungry?"

I leapt the last four feet and dusted off my pants. "Miig, it's really weird. You should see the …"

He cut me off, "Let's talk about that up front here, French. No need to bother everyone."

"But it's so …"

"French, up front with me. Chi-Boy, take the back. Everyone, grab your stuff." He was stern now, back to his order-barking tone. Chi-Boy slipped off the trail to reappear in behind the twins. He was used to obeying.

I shrugged back into my pack and dragged my feet to follow Miig, upset that I had news I couldn't share, especially with Rose, who looked at me now with curious dark eyes. I could have dragged that story out for a mile at least, could have spoken in a low voice so I'd have to stay close to her ear. Maybe even thrown an arm over her shoulder. Frigging Miig, so bossy. RiRi and Slopper were right, who died and made this guy Chief? Wanted all the info for himself first.

I stomped up beside Miig, who kept a few yards to the front.

"Tell me."

"I saw smoke and stuff."

"What stuff?"

"Trees moving and something yellow under the smoke."

"Where?"

"West."

He didn't ask anything more for a full two minutes and we walked in silence.

"Minerva was feeding her new grandson when the Recruiters busted into her home. They took the baby, raped her, and left her for dead. They answered to no one but the Pope himself, back then."

I unintentionally slowed down, so shocked I couldn't make my feet move with proper cadence. That shock froze into anger, and I sped back up directly beside Miig. He continued.

"Wab was alone for two whole years before she came to us. For the last six weeks of that time, she followed us in the trees, unable to trust that we wouldn't hurt her too. I knew she was there, I could see her peeking closer at night when she thought we were asleep."

I said nothing, thinking of the story she'd shared with us at Four Winds.

"Both RiRi and Slopper first came to us with a parent each. Both of them lost them to the schools later on. RiRi was just a baby when her mother was dragged off. Slopper, his dad went crazy one night, running straight into a Recruiter camp before we could stop him."

"Stop," I whispered.

He took a few more strides. "Tree and Zheegwon, they were held by a colony of townspeople who tried different ways to extract their dreams, figuring they'd found some kinda personal reservoir with Indian twins."

I tried to picture the serious white people as we'd come to know them, in their suits and hard briefcases and closely cropped hair. It was hard to imagine them getting excitable.

"We found them tied up in a barn, dangling like scarecrows from a rope thrown over a beam." He sighed, paused for another breath. "They were full of holes that'd been stitched up with rough thread, all up and down their sides. And with a pinky missing on each hand. They were seven then."

I wanted to throw up. I felt the bile burn at the base of my throat. This was my family. I didn't want to know all of this. I couldn't take anymore.

"Stop. Please." I could barely get the words out.

"I lost my husband in the schools. We were taken there together."

"Isaac?" I asked, remembering my father's first meeting with Miig.

He nodded, wincing at bit at the name like a remembered wound pinching at a nerve. He rubbed the marriage tattoo he shared with Isaac, a story he'd told us when RiRi had asked about the black outline of a buffalo on the back of his left hand.

"That's my wedding ring. Isaac had the same."

He slowed a bit, wavering off to the side, nearer to the trees, reaching out to lean against a birch as he paused. I stopped begging for him to stop.

MIIGWANS' COMING-TO STORY

ISAAC WAS A kind man, too kind really, for his own good. We'd made it out to our cottage. It was far enough in the bush that we knew we could manage there for at least a season or two before anyone even thought to come this way. It was deep winter when we arrived. We drove our Jeep to the main road and then parked it a few meters in. Then we unhitched quads from the pull and made our way to the cabin. It was still early days — all rumors and speculation — so we probably weren't as careful as we should have been. Still, we felt safe out there.

It used to be Isaac's grandfather's hunting camp. Over the years since the wedding, we'd fixed it up and put on an addition, taking down the smoker and installing a greenhouse. We were completely off the grid, which worked out perfectly since the power to remote areas had been cut long ago.

We had an uneventful three months, cut off but still together. Isaac was a poet, you see, and in the adversity the words kept coming. In some ways we were still happy. Isaac had his words, both English and Cree, and I had my Isaac.

Then one night, we heard a commotion in the bush.

"Mimi, we should go check. Could be game?" Isaac was cautiously hopeful. It was infectious. So far we'd managed to grab less than a dozen rabbits and only a skinny deer. What a day that one was — we resurrected an old ceremony for that deer. The smaller re-wilded breeds that people were living on, hamsters and cats, hadn't herded this far into the bush yet.

We took the rifle and went out to check, snowshoes on the deep snow, soft shuffle and silence. It was so quiet out here any noise carried. We walked across the expanse of what we considered our yard, then through a thin collection of birch to the tool shed. In a clearing, two hundred feet from the shed, were three people — a man, a woman, and another, younger woman. We watched from the trees for a bit. Only the younger one had a look I recognized. She was obviously Cree, but looked more plains than northern, so she was far from home. The others, I wasn't sure. They were dark, but they were speaking too low and in English, so I couldn't grab an accent or slang to place them.

Isaac looked at me, eyebrows arched. I knew what he was thinking. He had a soft spot for strays. I think that's why he took a chance on me to begin with, a long-haired hunter who'd wandered into North Town at the same time he was breezing through, reading from his latest book at a number of libraries and the few bookstores still scattered about. It was about the time literature was going through a bit of a renaissance, people clinging to that old adage about bedtime stories and the dreams they might bring. Isaac was unafraid of the rumors being thrown around about new factories where experiments were held and the danger that was coming. It was more because he felt he had value as a poet than the fact that he was a pale, green-eyed half-breed — and he did. But he overestimated how long that would last. And how quickly people would forget the art in the Indian and instead see only the commodity.

"We should stay alone." It was barely a whisper.

"They'll stumble on the cottage anyway. They're too close now."

I rolled my eyes. There was no use trying to talk him out of anything once he'd made up his mind.

When we came into the clearing, gun raised, they jumped and hastily greeted us in stumbling Anishnaabe, all except the second female, who must have been in her early twenties. She lifted her hood to cover her head and throw her face in shadows. The older woman yanked it back down and pulled her to her feet, apologizing for her rudeness.

Right away they smelled that Isaac was the kinder one and directed all their chatter to him.

"Oh, brother, I tripped on a log back that way. Really messed up my ankle." He bent down to rub at it, wincing as he did. "I was like, miigwetch, thanks a lot for that. Geez."

The man limped about to gather the few items they'd started to unpack, already guessing Isaac would extend the inevitable invitation.

"Yes, holy. I'm just exhausted. My binoojiing won't let up and give me rest and I feel crampy." The older woman arched her back and rubbed her rounded belly. I thought she just looked chubby; she was too soft and even all around.

"My husband is a healer. He can have a look at you both," Isaac said proudly, placing a hand on my shoulder. I sighed.

"No, no." The man was loud. "I'll be okay, just a bit of a twist. And my wife, well, she's just a complainer. First baby and all …"

The girl stayed quiet, lips tight, eyes to the ground.

We carried the man's packs and he hopped along with an arm thrown over his wife's shoulders. I should have guessed then from the softness of the canvas on the backpack, like it was brand new from the store, the way it was only one-layer kind of wet and not soaked through and frozen stiff in the snow. I should have guessed from the way he wasn't meticulous about packing up and almost left behind a precious tin of canned meat, like it was nothing. Like he could grab more at any time. The girl dragged along behind.

"You can stay until your ankle gets better," Isaac offered.

"Shouldn't take longer than a day," I remarked, throwing the too-light packs on the floor of the front hall. Isaac squeezed the back of my elbow in the dark.

"A day or two," I amended. But only because I loved my husband.

"We appreciate it," the woman said. "What with me being in this condition and all. Any time inside helps."

They slept in our spare room, all three of them, even though we offered the youngest the pullout couch in the front room. In fact, she was never left alone, the older woman even milling about in the hallway outside the bathroom when she went in. And I couldn't get a straight answer on how she knew them. Over soup that afternoon she said they were her cousins. But in the evening in front of the fire, while he nursed a glass of our rare whiskey (he asked for a second glass even, how rude), the man told Isaac she was his wife's sister. And she always seemed skittish ... scared, maybe.

"Oh, Mimi, you're so suspicious," Isaac told me that night under our duvet, the weight of his calf over my ankle. "You'd be skittish too if we were on the run in the woods."

I knew he was right. I tried to be more hospitable. But still, something kept me alert to discomfort. I was up and in the kitchen long before anyone else stirred, watching the snow fall in slow motion flakes in the yard.

The second day passed without remark. The trio slept late, wolfed down more of our lunch offering than was polite, and then retreated for an afternoon nap. Dinner found Isaac straining to make conversation over spaghetti and bannock while our guests glared at each other and watched the windows.

Something woke me up in the middle of the night. I lay in bed for a while, listening to Isaac breathe and the wind knot around the bare branches outside. I walked out into the hallway half lit by the moonlight falling in through the small, curtain-less window at the end and banged straight into the girl. She'd been standing in the shadows by our door.

"Oh, I'm sorry. Didn't see you there." I apologized but then grew angry. What in the hell was she doing by our door in the middle of the night? "How long …"

She pushed a calloused finger along my lips, and I shut up. "I can't do this no more. You and your man gotta run."

I pushed her hand away from my face, noticing the way it shook. "What do you mean, we gotta run? This is our home. We don't have to do anything."

That's when she pulled up her pant leg and I saw the black ankle monitor, blinking red in the dark like a buoy. That's also when the man came out into the hallway and saw us, then the blinking light laid bare and in plain sight. He yelled in a language I later found out was Tagalog, and the older woman rushed into the hallway. She grabbed at the younger woman by her braid, cursing in her language and dragging her back to their room.

"She's crazy. She doesn't know what she's talking about." The man laughed nervously. He shrugged his shoulders and took a few steps towards me, steps that were unencumbered by the limp that had made him a useless guest who couldn't help gather wood or leave with his odd family in tow.

Isaac was behind me now. The struggling woman yelled from the room now, "Run! You have to run, now! They're already on the way!"

There came the sound of struggle and a crash. The man backed down the hallway in a hurry and ducked in the open door before slamming it shut. I could hear the bolt being slid into place, and then a racket of furniture banging and panicked dialogue.

I wanted to kick down the door, ask a thousand questions, make them pay for bringing all this into our beautiful home with our books and the fireplace we'd built out of dry river rocks. But I knew we didn't have time. I knew then the rumors were true and we had precious little time to get our Indigenous asses out of the house and into the shadows.

I grabbed Isaac by the hand and brought him to our room. I pushed a chair against the doorknob in case those maniacs came for us themselves and pulled the bags out of the walk-in. "We'll take all the ammunition we can find. We can take the quads. They're loud, but we can get further into the bush with them. I'll grab the camping gear from under the stairs. Might be roughing it for a few weeks before we can find another livable spot. Maybe we can even circle back in a bit."

Isaac snapped out of his tired shock and began stuffing some precious books and the more beautiful of his sweaters into a duffel bag. But it was too late. The vans pulled up outside, and our guests hollered at them from their bedroom window, "Upstairs. Two males. Second door on the right."

Isaac was at the window before me and covered his open mouth with a hand. "Holy shit ..."

I squeezed in beside him. Outside the sky was full of lights, blue and red reflecting off the clouds and the trees and the sides of our cottage. Five Arctic Cat quads were parked, lengthwise and haphazard, out front, and men, all wearing identical white parkas with round, red logos were scattering about the yard.

"Isaac, just leave the bags. Get your shoes on now. Layer up as much as you can, hurry." I pushed him away from the window.

"Mi, it's too late. If I can just talk to them, I'm sure ..."

"They won't listen. You need to get ready to leave right this minute." I watched half the men circle to the back. We'd have a shot if we got to the cellar and came up into the yard. It wasn't a guarantee with all these men, but it was the best chance we had.

Isaac slid a hand across my shoulders, and I turned away from the window. He had that look of calm resolve on his face, the look he'd gotten when the dog had to be put down and when fire took our apartment in North Town.

"I really need you to trust me on this. This is our home. They can't just come in here and do what they like. Now, I'm not sure what all of this is really about, but that stuff we heard? Miigwans, that's just too ridiculous to be true."

I heard a sharp rap on the front door, and my heart jumped into my throat. Isaac didn't have memories in his family of the original schools, the ones that pulled themselves up like wooden monsters coming to attention across the land back in the 1800s — monsters who stayed there, ingesting our children like sweet berries, one after the other, for over a hundred years. Isaac didn't have grandparents who'd told residential school stories like campfire tales to scare you into acting right, stories about men and women who promised themselves to God only and then took whatever they wanted from the children, especially at night. Stories about a book that was like a vacuum, used to suck the language right out of your lungs. And I didn't have time to share them, not now.

"Isaac, I need you to run. Right now. We need to get the hell out of here, because those men down there —" I pointed behind me out the window "— they sent strangers into the woods to find us. Now they're surrounding our home in the middle of the night. Does that sound like they might be reasonable to you?"

We didn't have time to come to an agreement. The front door banged open and heavy footsteps were on our wooden stairs. I pushed Isaac behind me and squared my shoulders, wishing we'd started sleeping with the shotgun, like we'd talked about. If I had honestly known what was in store for us, I would have used it to finish us both, right then and there.

FINDING DIRECTION

"SOMETIMES, FRENCH, YOU gotta trust that people are making decisions for the better of the community based on things they know that you don't." He spoke softer now. "They're building a new school. I knew it was going up this way, but not where exactly. They know our people are moving north into the heavy forests and rocky earth. They aim to bring heavier manpower and facilities this way to shorten the transport time for those of us who get caught."

Holy shit. It was a construction site. They were building another school.

"But not everyone needs to know that right now. Sometimes, you have to not bring things into the open, put them aside so that people have the hope to put one foot in front of the other."

We walked side by side for another twenty minutes. I couldn't bear to look behind us at our ragtag family as they shuffled along, Slopper and the twins singing what we pretended was a warrior song to measure out time on the trail.

"About ten kilometers to the northwest of here," I said to Miig.

"I'd say the site is about a half-kilometer total size. The trees were coming down pretty fast. There must be a big group or large equipment or both to be moving at that pace." I tried to remember every detail, to unburden and inform at the same time, not envying Miig's role any longer. Missing the innocence of an hour ago when my only concern was touching the hand of a girl I thought I might love.

"Good job, my boy. Good job."

That night we set up camp on a flat stretch of field in the midst of tall pines and ate a good dinner of canned beans and a couple of ground birds roasted on our new hibachi. Minerva was delighted by the contraption and even taught us a new word, all of us, not just the girls.

We were sitting around the hibachi, feeling all modern and posh. I weaseled my way beside Rose, who had RiRi in her lap. RiRi was cleaning her new boots with spit and a finger.

"Abwaad." Minerva pointed to the birds on the grill.

"Abwaad? Is that a bird?" Rose asked.

That made her chuckle. "No, no. Abwaad. Cooking on a fire."

I put my head down on my bent knees and repeated it over and over as softly as I could, hoarding something precious. "Abwaad, cooking on a fire."

After we'd picked the bones clean and stored them in a canvas sack to boil for soup the next day, when we were all nestled in our blankets and allowing exhaustion to make the decisions, Miig spoke. "Tomorrow we turn east, northeast. For a bit, anyway. There might be more people up that way. Seems like the forest fires are in the west."

No one objected. Northeast or northwest, it didn't really make a difference. It was all north and it was all more days of walking.

I lay awake longer than even Chi-Boy that night, long enough to
see him slip the white trapper hat under Wab's pillow and linger
to touch her long hair as she slept.

I wanted to know the rest, wanted the story of Miigwans'
escape, because I thought just by knowing about it, somehow, it
would make our escape seem all the more plausible. But I couldn't
ask. It didn't take a genius to realize that Isaac was lost to the
schools, that Miig was alone and heartbroken. He'd lost someone
he'd built a life with right in the middle of that life. Suddenly, I
realized that there was something worse than running, worse
even than the schools. There was loss. I'd wait for him to tell
me the rest in his own time, if that ever even came. I fell asleep
watching the rise and fall of Rose's breaths and tried to imagine
us in another time, building instead of running.

THE POTENTIAL OF CHANGE

MIIG WAS WRONG about that last gust of winter. A week later and we were on our fifth day of constant snow. It was the kind of wet snow that's almost rain and hits you heavy. Minerva was in the hitch now almost permanently, banging on its side with an open palm when she had to get out to take a bathroom break. RiRi rode in there with her a bit, but Wab tried to keep her walking.

"It's warmer that way. Besides, you need to build your legs up. You're not a baby anymore."

No one was really talking much, we were too busy concentrating on staying upright and mobile and warm. Between us we wore every piece of clothing we had, Tree and Zheegwon taking turns with their baseball cap every hour. Still, Slopper's nose ran constantly and Miig had a cough that rattled around in his throat when he tried to hide it. Something had to change, and soon.

And then one day it did. Forever.

IT WAS NEARING dusk, not that the sky revealed anything other than a thick, wet fog, and we were preparing the ground to start setting up camp.

"Wab, I found a toy!"

RiRi's pink boots squelched and sucked in the ground mush. She'd given up trying to keep them spotless and they were speckled and streaked with hard mud.

Wab didn't look up. She was laying out the tarp that would keep the wet from our bones, but not the freeze. "Okay then, go play with it."

RiRi ran off to show Minerva, who sat in the cart like a queen on a rickety throne. I was on the other side of the clearing, putting up the string of bells that we used as an alarm system, when she yelled.

"Majan! Mudbin!"

Miig was the first one to the cart, where Minerva had propped herself up on her knees, her eyes wide. She handed something blue to Miig.

"I want it!" protested RiRi. "I found it."

I walked over to the cart with the others.

Miig was holding a plastic lunch pail with a broken hinge. On the front was the half-torn, waterlogged image of a man wearing a blue suit with a wide red cape. He was flying over buildings, but I couldn't make out much more through the wear. We'd found other junk out here. But when he opened the top I saw the reason for concern. Inside was a half a piece of bread wrapped in clear plastic. It wasn't even mouldy yet.

"Could be the same group Wab saw back before the resort." He rubbed his chin then gave orders.

"Chi-Boy, walk the perimeter. Tree, Zheegwon, lay extra wires."

He turned to me. "French, you know what to do."

I jogged to the trees, found the best specimen to hold my weight, and ascended. We all knew what was up: we'd found other evidence of travelers, and Miig's first priority was to keep us safe. I got excited every time, hoping that we'd run into some friendlies, maybe even someone we knew from before. In the five years I'd been with my group, we'd found others only seven times, and each time we'd parted after several days. It was safer to be small, to be less of a disturbance for the Recruiters to track.

The landscape had started to change, and here and there amongst the green were slashes of black where the Precambrian rock grafted sharp hills and cut into craggy cliffs. We did our best to avoid them when we were on the move. Shifting rocks with sudden drops were dangerous. And the incline was tough on us all, especially with the cart to pull. I saw a ridge of solid black cut through the forest like a vein. We were definitely getting more north now. I wasn't up there for long before I saw them: two figures, huddled around an open fire in a small clearing about a three-hour march to the west. One was wearing camouflage; the other, foolishly, wore a bright red hat.

Miig was talking with Minerva, who was still in the wagon, low and serious. Her face was smooth with stress, and she looked as coherent as I'd seen her in a while. Miig's hair was tucked up into a grey woolen toque, and with the wide grey scarf wrapped around his neck several times so that his entire mouth was obscured, he looked much older. Rose stood up from where she was playing tic-tac-toe with RiRi in a crust of snow with a couple of sticks, but I went over to the Elders first.

"I saw them."

"Where?" Miig and Minerva turned their whole attention on

me, and I slowed down to tell my report right.

"West. Three, maybe four hours' walk, maybe a bit more with the wagon. Two people. Couldn't tell who they were, but I didn't see any vehicles so they're probably not Recruiters."

"You don't know that for sure. It's dangerous to make assumptions."

"No, but they just didn't seem like it." I felt stupid and very young. "I mean, they were kind of hanging out around a fire."

"A fire? This early? And where you could see it?"

I nodded. Miig squinted his eyes and tilted his head back so that his scruffy chin popped out of the scarf. "That's odd. An early evening fire? And in the open?"

I nodded again, not sure if he was really asking a question.

"Recruiters might be that clumsy, but then, if they're out this far, they're hunting for sure. Got to be stealthy to sneak up on Indians."

Wab joined the circle. "Two of them? One bigger than the other? One in a red hat?"

"Yeah."

She exchanged glances with Miig. "That's them."

"Maybe they're townies," Tree piped up from behind me. Zheegwon got pale at the thought of it, took off the baseball cap, and fit it onto his brother's head. The twins often reverted to small acts of care between the two of them when they were anxious. They hadn't heard about Wab's sighting, having already gone to bed that night at the fire.

"Could be ..." Miig was already looking into the trees for Chi-Boy. I could see the jump of adrenaline in his facial muscles.

RiRi wandered over with her tic-tac-toe stick still in her hand. "Maybe they're kids. Just dumb kids that don't know better,

Miig. On account of they got no grown-ups."

We stood around the wagon in silence, until Wab spoke up. "I think it's worth checking."

Chi-Boy stepped out of the bush, and Miig made his decision. "We camp tonight. Tomorrow we keep walking east." Almost as an afterthought he said, "And we'll see whatever there is to see." Then he started unloading the gear for the night.

We woke up early, as usual, and immediately started the pack-up while Wab and Rose boiled water for the mush and got the youngest and oldest set for the day. We moved at the same speed, just with an alternate set of steps. There was a different potential to today, and we could feel it. Today we might catch up to the strangers. Today we might make new friends or fall prey to new enemies. A few weeks ago Tree and Zheegwon had told the story of cannibal people while the fire died down. I hadn't been able to shake it yet.

"They're the wiindigo people, those who need to eat but can only eat human flesh."

"They lost their way but don't want to get back on the path. All they want is meat."

"And they don't care if it's their own children, they'll eat them just the same."

Chi-Boy shut it down early. "All right, all right. We don't need no one screaming out in their sleep now. Let's call it a night."

Now here we were, ready to walk towards the unknown. What if these two strangers in the woods were wiindigo people? What if their early fire right out in the open was for cooking up a third stranger who wandered across their path?

"Mush?"

"Ah, Jesus." I hadn't heard Rose's footsteps, and her voice in my ear startled me to curse. "Sorry, Rose. Uh, no, I'm good." I waved away the bowl she held out. "Give mine to Slopper."

She sat down beside me on the rolled-up tent where I perched, distracted in my packing. She handed me the tin bowl anyway, and I took a mouthful. We all needed to eat in the morning. It was dangerous to run out of steam on the walk. "What's up?" She was kind in the question, without her usual edge and defense.

"Not sure, really." I swallowed the warm porridge and took another bite, thinking of what was really going on in my head. I reverted to the books I loved, those rare and impractical luxuries I'd happened on a few times in my life and hoarded until they fell apart, all pulp and tears.

"It's weird when you come to a spot in the story where the plot could go either way, you know?"

She just stared. Maybe she wasn't a big reader.

"It's just, when you could go one direction and have life turn out one way, or go another direction and have life be completely a different way, it's nerve-wracking."

She nodded. "I know. Imagine if I'd gone west instead of north when I left my uncle. I'd have never found you. I mean, any of you guys."

I flushed hard and shoved more mush into my mouth to break up the smile that pushed its way onto my face.

We sat in silence while I finished the bowl. The ground was still frozen and the warmth of another body so close was comforting. The air stung your nose on the inhale and there was water-smoke at the exhale. But the frost wasn't as thick and the last of the snow was melting into crust. Soon enough the woods would begin to get dressed for spring.

CHI-BOY MUST HAVE started out ahead before the sun rose because now he came jogging back into the circle of our half-packed tents.

"An hour's walk." He pointed his hand into the bush. The men. After three days' time, we were gaining on them. Miig was cautious and slow, but he kept us on a path to intercept the two figures I'd been watching again from the treetops before bedtime, checking for anything unusual, trying to piece together their schedule and motives. So far I'd gotten nothing except that they seemed to have an abundance of food, gauging by the intensity and timing of their fires, and that they didn't seem to be on the run, taking their time and even staying at one site for two nights instead of one. Two nights would get you killed if the Recruiters were on your trail.

Miig sighed, looked around at the tops of the trees with his hands on his hips, and said, to all of us and to no one in particular, "Today's the day."

THE OTHER INDIANS

BY NOON, WE'D caught up to them. They were lazy and messy, and we'd walked over more blatant tracks and litter than we'd seen for months. And today they hadn't even bothered to pack up and walk. Instead, when Chi-Boy and I made it to the perimeter of their campground, they were dicking around. The tall Nish, with broad shoulders and long thin hair pulled back into two scraggly braids under his red hat, was carving a small piece of wood, leaning back in a folding chair against a tree. The other man, dressed in head to toe camouflage that did him no good lying on the ground by the small fire, seemed to be napping, his brimmed camo hat pulled down over his face. What could they possibly be waiting around for?

We reported back to Miig, who waited with the group a little further out.

"I don't like it. Let's stick together, and make sure the girls are in sight at all times." He spoke to the two of us alone. When he mentioned keeping the girls safe, I looked over at Rose, who stood by Minerva's trailer holding RiRi's hand. Chi-Boy kept his eyes on Wab for the rest of the conversation.

"Chi-Boy, you keep your knife at the ready. And French?" He handed me one of the two rifles we possessed. "This is loaded for now, and it will stay that way until we get past these two and back out on our own."

I nodded and shouldered the gun. I was comfortable with it, we all were. Miig had made sure of it. I could shoot a squirrel off a branch if I had to, though there wouldn't be enough meat left for a toddler. I'd figured that one out the hard way.

We joined the rest.

"Well, the strangers are just past those pines. We can't rightly avoid them, and we have an obligation to see who they are and if they need help. Or if maybe one of us knows one of them from before. But if they are true strangers, we need to keep moving. And if they are more than strangers, if they turn out to be danger, we need to think of each other and ourselves first. We have to."

Miig's tone spread a look of anxiety among the group, all except for RiRi, who looked excited.

"Are they kids, French?" Her little voice got high pitched.

"Nah, Ri. They're grown-ups. Two men."

"Oh." She kicked at the ground in her muddy pink rubbers. "Maybe they got kids somewhere else, though, eh? Maybe that's where they're going."

"Sure, Ri. Maybe."

Wab pulled her over and squeezed her in tight so that her toque slipped down over her eyes to the bridge of her nose. The little girl smiled in the embrace.

"Okay, then, let's head over. I'll take the front with French, regular formation, Chi-Boy at back." We assembled under his instruction and pushed into the bush.

We were two rows back when a man yelled out, "Who's there?"

Miig and I exchanged silent looks. It wasn't that we'd been discovered that made us wary, it was that they were confident enough to call out. What if we were Recruiters? What if we were deranged townies? And what if, by chance, we were game that could feed them? Who would take such a chance? I picked up more of Miig's anxiety about the strangers.

Miig stood to his full height and pulled at the strap of his gun so that it swung around his body; he held it in both hands, pointing into the clearing.

"Ahneen?"

Silence.

"Aandi wenjibaayan?" Miig asked where they were from. Playing Indian geography meant you could figure out who was who before you even saw them. And for Miig, I could see why it was doubly important to establish nationhood.

Silence. Then the reply came from a second voice. "Boozhoo. Anishnaabe?"

"Mmmm. Niin Miigwans nindizhinikaaz." Miig moved slowly forward, introducing himself and asking for a name in return. "Aaniin ezhinikaazoyan?"

"Niin Travis nindizhinikaaz."

Mumbling from their end and then another voice: "Lincoln, from Hobemma Nation, out west. Tansi." The second man, the one who had called out to us at first, answered in English and then greeted Miig in Cree. All the while, Miig slowly crept forward. I stayed in the space left between him and the group.

Miig turned back to us and motioned us forward with his head, still holding the gun at waist height.

"I'm coming into the clearing. I have nine others with me."

"Uh-huh."

"Okay." He broke through the last row with us just behind him and entered the clearing.

The tall, long-haired man was standing beside the fire, his chair and wood abandoned behind but the knife still in his ham fist. The shorter camo man stood a little in front, his hat pulled back now to reveal a scraggly mustache and small eyes. He looked a bit younger than Miig and addressed him as older brother.

"Ahneen, Nisaye." He stepped forward, and the pair shook hands. Then he stepped back and pointed to his companion. "This here is Lincoln." Lincoln just nodded, then turned and threw his knife so that it stuck into the tree behind his chair. He was less than interested.

"This is my family." Miig held his hand out to us and we approached in a bundle. "My boys Zeegwan, Tree, French, Slopper, and Chi. My daughters Wab, Rose, and RiRi. And Nokomis Minerva."

"Ahneen, Nokomis." The man named Travis bowed at the waist to Minerva, who giggled and swiveled her hips a bit. She was as delighted with the introduction as she was with the melodic sounds of her language sprinkled over the woods, even if the words were said clumsily and even out of order at times. If I hadn't been flooded with adrenaline and worry I would have mouthed each one after it was said, shoving them into my pockets like sweets to suck on later.

"Ten. That's a pretty big family. Lucky man, Nisaye." Travis looked us all over once and then back again, like he was assessing us. When his eyes got to Wab they grew bigger, and his smile faltered, but he recovered quickly.

"Uh-huh." Miig was still cautious. "Well, we're heading through this way, so we won't get in your way, here."

I turned to look at Wab. Her one eye was so narrow I would have thought it was closed shut if not for the glint in there.

"Stay for food. Our hunt was good." He was eager to move away from Wab's glare and took a few steps towards the fire. He pointed to a cauldron hanging over the fire on an old lead pipe. "Venison stew." He picked up two sticks that were lying in the pit. Each one had clumps of browning dough caught on the bark. "Bread."

My mouth filled with water. Slopper exclaimed out loud, "Oh my Jesus!"

"We don't want to take your supplies. We'll manage." Miig had released the gun when he shook hands, and it hung at his side. When he pulled the strap to realign it on his back, I shouldered my own. I wasn't sure if he'd picked up on Wab's reaction to the man. I was a bit distracted by the smells and the thought of the food, to be honest. I pleaded in my head to be allowed to stay but knew better than to say anything out loud. I wasn't one of the kids anymore.

"No, no. Don't be thick. There's enough or I wouldn't have offered. Lincoln and I were just in Espanola and grabbed some supplies. We're stocked."

Now I knew we had a shot at staying. Miig thrived on information, and if these two had just been in a town, they had info that we might need and that Miig would want to hear.

"Okay," he agreed. We all sighed behind him, relieved. "But we smoke my tobacco tonight."

"Nishin." Travis laughed and poked at the pot while we unloaded and took up seats around the fire. Wab refused to sit, standing behind Miig with her arms folded across her chest.

Chi-Boy slipped off unnoticed, and I knew he was scouting the area in case we had to leave in a hurry. I felt foolish, sitting in the warmth with the Elders and the kids. I wanted to be of use too.

"Be right back," I mumbled to Tree and stood up.

The one introduced as Lincoln had returned to his chair outside of the circle around the pit. It was him who called out to me. "Hey, boy."

"Just going for a piss." I wasn't sure why, but the large man made me feel nervous. "Don't wanna do it out in the open." I gave a forced chuckle. He lowered his eyebrows and turned back to his carving, shaking his head slightly. I hope the others hadn't heard. I didn't want to sound weak in front of Rose, like some sweaty little kid who can't take care of his family.

I slipped into the first row of trees, in the same spot we had entered from, then I walked left, keeping an eye on the clearing. It turned out that the fire and the men's tents and chairs were in a small circular patch at the end of a long, narrow clearing so that the whole spot was kind of in the shape of a spoon. At the top of the handle, the space dropped off with one of those craggy cliffs of shale rock. I crept to the edge as close as I could manage and peered over. It was about a six-storey drop. With the pointed edges and rough landing, there was no surviving that fall.

"What're you doing?"

I jumped, grasping a low, sticky pine branch beside me for balance. I didn't actually pitch forward, but the sudden movement this close to the drop made my head swim. I swung around.

"Tabernacle, Chi-Boy! You scared the life outta me."

He smiled a little bit and then reeled it back in. "Sorry. What're you looking for?"

"Nothing." I was a bit defensive. Why did I have to be looking for anything in particular? Why couldn't I be altruistically scouting like him? "Just looking, is all." I bit the pine gum off my fingers.

"Let's get back." He slipped into the trees on the other side and started to weave his way back.

He stopped. "Hey, did you notice the way that guy looked at Wab? I think he remembered her."

It was weird that he would be asking me this. Chi-Boy was not much of a talker. "Yeah, yeah, I did. He's kinda nervous about her."

Chi-Boy nodded his head, pulling his lips together tight. "Let's keep an eye on that."

I nodded back, copying the way he held his mouth. Yes, we would definitely do so. Us men. We'd be vigilant. Chi-Boy turned and started making his way through the trees. I watched him for a minute, and tried to listen. There was nothing — the absence of sound was the only thing the ear picked up. There was no doubt Chi-Boy was the best scout we had, probably the best scout anyone had. I followed close behind, imitating his movements.

Miig had told us once about how bats moved. "They're blind. That's why they say 'blind as a bat.' So they send out these waves of sound, to see what they bounce off of. Then they know where they can fly, where they can fit."

Chi-Boy used his arms as sound, pushing them out in front of him and then following through with his shoulders. His feet went last, so that by the time he'd moved his upper body forward he could watch the ground for exactly where his feet should land with minimal impact and sound. I imitated his movement. It felt like swimming through the woods, my arms fleshy paddles against the cold air currents. Time went quickly like this, moving as fluid.

Soon we cut out into the clearing, a few feet from where Lincoln sat in his chair, still carving a stick into nothing more exciting than a sharp point. He threw his head back, swallowing something small from his cupped palm. He jumped when we moved into sight.

"Pissing in pairs?" He snorted when we approached. We had startled him and it hurt his pride. Neither one of us answered, but I couldn't help but smirk a bit at having managed to sneak up on the older man.

We joined the circle around the fire. Evening was coloring in the sky from the corners, navy over cerulean. I was casual about finding space beside Rose, and Chi-Boy slipped in beside Miig. I caught him mumbling near Miig's ear a few times, the Elder pretending not to hear anything other than the jibber-jabber of Travis as he recounted the pair's uneventful travel.

"Yeah, we've pretty much seen nothing but bunnies and buzzards since we left town. Came across the buck just yesterday out of sheer luck."

"How's Espanola holding up? Not many towns left up this way, I reckon." Miig dug for information we could use.

"Nah, that's for sure. I think it might be the last in this region. But she's still going." He paused to fish more bread out of the fire and handed two clumps to Rose and me. I had planned to turn it down and offer my share to the girls, but the smell hit me in the stomach, so hard I couldn't make words.

Travis finished off the roll-your-own he'd gotten from Miig and spoke through his last deep exhale. "It's the schools. More and more construction, I guess. They're going up like weeds. Espanola is the link into the North for supplies and industry."

Miig smoked his roll slow. He paused to catch the last bit of

Chi-Boy's report, then responded. "I hear it's more than that. I hear Nish are putting up a bit of a resistance in Espanola."

What? I hadn't heard this before. Mind you, I wasn't yet privy to the private council of Miig and strangers when we ran into them. I was barely privy to Miig's council with Chi-Boy and even Minerva, though that would have been harder to access, seeing as how they counseled in the language.

Lincoln stopped carving and watched the men at the fire. Travis curled his back inward, a defensive movement of the young. In that space his voice was softer, like an echo of a man he used to be.

"There's a bit of a movement, I guess you'd call it. That's what they call it, anyway. They're camped out by the town, and they're armed. They haven't been hauled in yet. But it's only a matter of time before the schools take care of the easy pickings and go after the ones putting up a fight."

"They're up there acting like frigging woodlands wizards." Lincoln raised his voice to join in from his pace outside of the circle. "It's stupid is what it is. Time's a-wasting. You either run or you find other ways to fit in and get by. Ain't no use in holding on to ways that are dead. It just brings death closer."

"And what other ways could we fit in? Isn't running towards something other than this all we have?" Miig threw back. "Or am I missing something?" He had an edge to his voice that made me check the gun was within quick reach.

There was a pause. I put my fingers around the handle and swung it closer. Chi-Boy unfurled and straightened to his full height behind Miig, who still sat beside Travis, calmly finishing his smoke. But his eyes were narrow and far away. I knew where he was. He was back at his old cottage with Isaac and the betrayers. He was remembering pain.

I had no time to check the others, watching the muscle twitch on Miig's jaw, observing the silent curl of Chi-Boy's spine. Taking in the tick and creak of Lincoln's chair as he slowly lowered himself from tilt. Hearing the breathing of Travis in the boney shell of his shoulders. All this in a dozen heartbeats that pushed against the collar of my flannel button-up.

Travis rebounded. "Hiding is all. That's what he means. Hiding and pretending you're not Indian. Some of the half-breeds can do it. Hell, some of the full-bloods, too." He pushed an elbow into Slopper's arm beside him, looking for an ally in his commentary to make it light. "Am I right? You seen some of those Mohawks. Eyes bluer than the sky, eh?"

Slopper managed a half smile that looked like he had gas and leaned away and into RiRi, who had fallen asleep near the warmth of the blaze, her belly full of stew.

Miig locked eyes with Lincoln, who in turn refused to look away. His was a face full of challenge and bravado. Again, it was Travis who pulled in the other direction.

"Me, I'm inclined to stay out in the bush. Cities, they bring nothing but the worst out in people."

Wab snorted and walked in a small circle, shaking her head. I know for sure Miig noticed this time.

"I've done some bad shit in my time in the cities. Years back I had some bad habits. The kind of habits that make a man do things he isn't proud of." He poked at the fire with a thin stick, more nerves than anything. "But I will say this, in my defense, not that I can defend myself, really —" here he looked up at Wab for the first time "— I never would have done things if I'da known the outcome. My intentions were never to get anyone hurt. I never raised a hand against anyone and wouldn't allow it."

She stepped back into the shadows, arms still folded. He went on.

"And I am a different man today, out of the damned city. I found Lincoln here leaving the city the same way. We teamed up and have stayed away from people since. It's better that way. Now that I know what people are capable of, why would I ever go back?"

"You couldn't." Slopper broke the tension. "None of us can. On account of the Recruiters. We're bush Indians for real now."

Travis laughed at Slopper's serious decree and clapped him on his thick back. "Well, I think now that we've eaten and smoked good offerings together, and seeing as how the sky is falling, you should consider just putting up here for the night." He opened his arm and gestured to the clearing. "We haven't heard a peep until you wandered by, and it's a good, sheltered spot. Ground's not too wet, didn't take on too much snow with these trees blocking drifts."

"No, no, we need to move on." But I could see in Miig's face that he was concerned about how far the day had gotten away from us. We had barely an hour before the dark tumbled down into every nook and cranny in these woods. And at this time of year, it was important to pick good spots to rest undernourished bones.

"Come on now, Nisaye. From this spot, the clearing goes back about three hundred feet until it hits a drop-off. It's secluded. You can take your clan further that way if you'd like. Or you can share the fire with us. Either way, me and Lincoln don't mind." He stood up, brushed off his backside, and clapped his sidekick on the shoulder. "Do we, Linc?"

The man didn't answer at first. His eyes had become glassy and his lips were too thick for clear speech. He reminded me of

Wab that day back at the Four Winds: distorted somehow. Travis squeezed his grip on the man and smiled real tight until he answered. "Frig! No, no. It's good. Stay wherever. The more neechies the better." He addressed Rose and Wab when he spoke next, something cloudy on his face. "Stay close by. It's safer the closer you are."

The girls turned their backs to him, not so much to ignore his veiled remark as to show him they had no fear of him. But you don't turn your back on a dangerous animal. Only squirrels should be able to see your spine. We didn't know that he was an animal we had yet to imagine could exist.

THE WAY IT ALL CHANGED

WE SET UP our tents in a semicircle, backing onto the woods, midway between their fire and the cliff. Miig didn't want to stay close, nor did he want to be backed up onto an impossible exit.

We built our own fire and unfurled blankets. Light rain fell for about an hour as the sun was setting so we roped up our tarps and sat together for a moment, to regroup and plan watch.

"We'll do hour shifts and leave at first light. Starting with Tree and ending with French. Got it?"

No one was sure later who was to blame that we were caught unaware, but then, the idea of blaming someone was too horrible to imagine. It would have killed us even more, and we were already so diminished.

I heard her at the same time I felt a body crash into the side of the tent, full weight hard on my back while I lay, still clothed, in my sleeping bag. The body gave a sound like a kitten squeezed too tight, a kind of windless yelp. The sound pushed adrenaline into my thighs and knocked sleep out of my head. I struggled under the weight and whoever it was rolled off, cursing.

I heard another yelp and then a screech, a long wail that made my teeth chatter. It was Wab.

"What the hell?" I pushed to my knees and unzipped the tent flap. I turned once to see Slopper, eyes wide, blankets tucked around his face like a giant baby. I saw in his eyes the reflection of the Morse code my heart was pushing out: terror.

About twenty feet off, Tree and Zheegwon were back to back, arms intertwined, at the end of a gun held by Travis. Miigwans was a few steps to their right, his own gun on the ground by his feet, chest heaving. I couldn't see Minerva or Rose, but Chi-Boy lay on the ground, his own knife pushed through his arm. Wab was still screaming, standing in front of her tent in her long underwear, mouth open in a round *O* of panic. At first I thought she must be screaming over Chi-Boy's wound, but then I followed her stare. Lincoln, having picked himself up from where he'd fallen into my tent, had lumbered over behind Travis. His hair was messy on top and his face looked dozy, like a sleepy child. He was swaying a bit.

I thought it was maybe drink, or whatever he'd been swallowing back at the campfire, that was making him move that way. But then he turned and I saw RiRi, her throat grasped under his thick arm, legs kicking the air. She was grabbing at his forearm with her little hands, her face bright red.

"Just put her down." Miig tried to keep his voice steady. "Please, just put the girl on the ground so she can breathe."

Travis licked his lips, shifting his weight between the balls of his feet. He tried keeping his eyes pinned on the twins, Miig, and Wab while he backed up.

"Linc," he called to his partner over his shoulder. "Linc, the girl is no good dead. For Chrissakes, man, make sure she's breathin'."

"Put her down!" Miig yelled now, pointing, an edge of panic in his voice.

"Easy, Chief. Easy." Travis trained his handgun on Miig and moved forward quickly to kick the hunting rifle away from reach and just into the shadows at the edge of the woods.

Then he turned, "Lincoln, for fucksakes, put her down!"

The bigger man obliged, bending his arm so that RiRi dropped suddenly to the ground. She would have fallen flat on her face if her arm weren't being held at a cruel angle. Instead she kind of hung there. At least her feet were on the ground and she was coughing now.

I hadn't been seen yet, still half in the farthest tent and with Lincoln's unobservant current state. I slowly pulled back through the flap, turning to show Slopper a finger pressed to lips. He hadn't moved. I reached beside my bag and retrieved the rifle. All the saliva dried up in my mouth.

"Linc, we got the 'cruiters coming any minute now. Every head is worth a fortune. Don't damage any of 'em."

They were traitors. Indians turning in Indians for reward. I couldn't believe it. I'd been lulled to complacency by the color of skin and an accent that made home feel real.

"She's hurt! Let her go!" It was Rose. She'd emerged from her tent and was holding Minerva back at the door. Minerva, who had seen RiRi dangling from the man's meaty grasp while her arm twisted at a sick angle, was frantic to claw past and into the clearing. The sight of the old woman in her kerchief and long skirts over track pants made Lincoln laugh. He dropped RiRi to clutch his belly, and that's when Travis turned his head and Chi-Boy made his move.

He jumped from his crouch on the ground, the knife out of

his arm and back in his hand. He lunged at Travis, driving the blade into the man's leg, just above the knee. The older man screamed and dropped the gun in pain and shock. Miig jumped at it, smashing a fist into the howling man's chin on the way back up.

Lincoln, watching the group start to rally, picked RiRi up and threw her over his wide shoulder. I didn't see a weapon on him, but just the sheer size of him matched with his unnatural state made him a danger to us all, especially for RiRi. He turned and started to run.

"Stop!" Miig yelled. "I'll shoot!"

But he wouldn't. The clearing was dark and RiRi was at risk. Instead Miig gave chase, Wab at his heels, quickly catching up and passing him, her old runner instincts returned. Rose followed. Behind her, Minerva jogged, her arms pumping at her sides, not going much faster than a walk, her lips pushed out like a Nish GPS system. While half the group took off after RiRi and the hulk, the twins had gathered up Chi-Boy, pulling him away from Travis, who was crumpled on the ground with a bloody mouth. Tree ran to my tent where I sat half in, half out.

"You okay, French?" He peered in behind me at Slopper. "Slopper?" He gave the boy the thumbs-up sign. Slopper just stared in return.

"We gotta tie this guy up quick, Tree." Zheegwon came up behind his brother.

I watched them tie Travis's hands to his ankles with a piece of rope before slinging my rifle on my back. Then I ran off into the dark after my family.

I ran hard, with abandon, into the narrow swatch of the clearing, darker here with the closer trees. I ran full out, almost tripping over the huddled shape of Minerva where she sat, crouched on the ground, rocking back and forth and muttering words I couldn't pick up. I managed to avoid her, but slammed my shoulder hard into a protruding birch branch. I heard a dry snap, and I wasn't sure if it had come from the branch or the explosion of heat in my arm or from further up the path. It didn't matter. I just kept going.

Up ahead I could see shadows and then figures as the trees opened and the moon poured into the clearing before the cliff. I slowed down to assess, like Miig had taught me to do. One of the figures was on the ground, another was bent over, hands on knees. The third was holding on to a tree, leaning over the edge.

And that was it.

There were only three.

I doubled my speed and burst into the moonlight. Wab was on the ground. She looked like she was sleeping, but her eyes were wide open. Rose was bent over, throwing up between her feet, hysterical in between retches. It was Miig who leaned over the edge. I grabbed him first, taking his forearm into my grip. It's a good thing, too, because his hand let go seconds later, too shaky to hold on. I pulled him back hard, and he fell on top of my legs on the grass.

"Where'd they go? Did we lose them?"

I refused to put the pieces together.

"Miig, move, get up." I struggled under his dead weight. "Miig, c'mon, we're giving him too much of a head start. I'll go into the bush on the west. You take the east side."

He wasn't moving. I got angry, pushed at him, kicking him in the back to dislodge my other foot from under him. Still, he was motionless.

"Come on, you guys!" I was yelling now, pacing a small half circle around the catatonic group. "Let's go! Do I need to do this alone?" I waited two seconds for an answer. "Fine, I'm going."

I walked between Miig and the cliff, on my way to into the trees where I'd mimicked Chi-Boy's stealth earlier on, like that meant anything. And then I saw it. A single pink boot, all shiny like candy, one of the fastest boots in the world, real nishin. And it was empty, on its side, at the edge of the cliff.

There is a feeling that has no name because, really, it is such an absence that it exists only in a vacuum of feeling and so, really, can have no name. It sucks you inside out and places you in a space where touch and taste and sound and sight all turn to ash. I was there now, alone. There was no mooring, no ground, no sky. There was just me and the boot, and then, suddenly, the warm weight of the rifle on my back.

My vision narrowed, and I turned on a heel, throwing myself back the way I came. From a thousand miles away I heard Miigwans call, "French! Come back." But it could have just been the wind.

I passed Minerva and the broken birch and I bounded over the ground, legs aching, the gun bouncing softly against my spine. Later, I couldn't recall this journey back to the camp. There was no planning, no ideas or theories or even any real rage locked inside my skull. There was just nothing. Nothing but a pink boot without a girl to wear it and a rifle that I knew as well as my own hand.

I crashed into the campsite, startling the twins, who had finished tying up Travis and were guarding him with the handgun. Slopper sat at the edge of the tent, the blankets still pulled tight around his cheeks.

"French! Jesus, you scared us." Tree trained the gun back at our prisoner from where he had pointed it at me and wiped his forehead with the back of a dirty hand, leaving a streak like paint. "Where're the others?"

"Did you get RiRi?" Zheegwon moved closer to his brother. I must have had it written all over my face, because he grabbed the baseball cap off Tree's head and pushed it over his own, eyes still on me.

"Frigging Linc. He killed her, didn't he? Dammit, I told him to lay off those pills." Travis spat blood into the grass and sighed. He struggled to his knees, hands pulled tight behind him, and looked up.

"Uh, listen, boy. There's no use in us fighting now."

I reached behind me and yanked on the strap, bringing the rifle to my side. I cocked the barrel and trained it on the prostrate man in front of me. Panic flashed across his face and then it settled into a look of soft, practiced pleading. That's the only time I felt anger through it all, seeing that rehearsed mask slip over his dark face.

"Hey now, come on. Let me go now and I can show the rest of you the way out of here, before the white boys show up." Blood and spit flew with his words, betraying his anxiety under the mask.

"French? French, it's okay, we got him under control." Tree was trying to reason with me. Or maybe it was just the wind.

I kept my eyes on Travis. He nodded at Tree's wisdom and then tried a weak smile at me. "Yeah, c'mon, Brother."

Time is slow in that vacuum space. In this new space, I had time to aim squarely between the man's eyes, watching his muscles contort and his skin wrinkle. Then I decided against it, lowering the barrel to his chest: always go for the sure target. Miig had taught us that on one of my first hunts, and I listen to my Elders.

I dug a shoe in to accommodate for the kick back and bent at the knee, just like Miig had showed me.

"Come on now! Don't be stupid, kid! We can get out of here. Let's go! Come on, kid! I didn't mean it! It's nothing personal!"

I heard him whine a little at the end of his plea. But then, maybe it was just the wind.

I pulled the trigger and the wind stopped blowing.

THE LONG STUMBLE

WE RAN. I can't really recall what the packing-up was like or if I even contributed, but we were gone from the clearing and into the darkest part of the woods before the sun was fully up.

I know I held on to the gun, still warm in my palm, for most of the run, up until we heard the whistles far away, echoing off that cliff, and I swung it back behind me and snapped out of it a bit, just enough to take whatever Rose had in her arms in addition to her pack and to run behind her to keep pace.

We ran for hours, Chi-Boy and Miig taking turns carrying Minerva like a child on their backs while she wailed and sang and mewled in cycles. We zigged and we zagged, and when he wasn't packing our distraught Elder, Chi-Boy was off leaving false trail leads for any potential followers, his arm held closed with duct tape since there was no time to properly stitch it up.

By evening we were exhausted. We'd run and mourned for hours, each one of us crying out when the image of RiRi came to mind. RiRi, in one shiny pink boot dropping off the edge of the rock, held to the body of her would-be kidnapper by the iron bar of his arm. Instead of a captor, he became her anchor, dragging her all the way to the bottom. Camp that night was two tents thrown up hastily in the middle of dense bush with the spring bugs newly awake buzzing at the tears we hadn't had time to repair. We slept with our shoes on, piled together like sticks, falling unconscious more than to sleep. Rose curled around me, but I could barely feel her. Something had changed since I'd fired the gun, since I'd killed Travis. It was like a color had ceased to exist and now the world seemed dull.

RiRi was dead. I had killed a man. And there was no taking either of those things back. For the first time in several years I missed my parents as physical pain at the bottom of my stomach and under each kneecap. That's where the loss lived, in those strangely normal spots on my body. I didn't think I deserved to rub them, so I fell into dreamless sleep with a throb and a pull in my body.

The next morning Wab made sure we each ate a bowl of lukewarm mush in the cold hour before the sky started shedding layers into a lighter blue. She spoon-fed Minerva, who was now unresponsive, and rag-washed her face and hands before taking her into the bush to pee and then bundling her back up. Her cart had been left back at the clearing, so she made a kind of sling to balance the woman's weight on Chi-Boy's back.

"A bit warmer now." Tree spoke to Zheegwon in whispers. They needed to hear each other's voices. It was part of their coping.

"It'll be full spring soon. Saw some green on the brown trees."

"That's good."

We didn't have much to pack up and soon we were on our winding path again, heading everywhere and nowhere, frantic to get away.

The next two days and nights were much the same. Tree
and Zheegwon commented on the weather getting warmer and
the bugs coming back. Minerva rode catatonic on our strongest
carriers, and I was numb.

It was the fourth day when Miig called to me from the front
of the line.

"French? Get up here, boy."

I made my way up while he waited. Before I would have rushed,
but now I wasn't sure I even wanted to join him. I wasn't really
sure of anything. I wasn't sure I even wanted to run anymore.
Maybe I could just sit and wait for the Recruiters to pick me
up. Maybe I could use the last bullet I had in my gun to just go away.

I fell in stride beside him. At first he said nothing.

"I didn't want to live after Isaac didn't make it out of the
school," he said. "I'd escaped, sure, but why? I had no life without
him. The only thing that kept me going was the promise I'd made
to myself to go back, to get Isaac the first chance I got.

"At first I had to run, of course. The second they realized the
laundry boy was no longer in the laundry room they would comb
the area. So I ran. For two days and two nights, in my bare feet and
a uniform that looked like men's pajamas. It's not as bad as it
sounds. At night I found nooks and holes to crawl into. And anything is better than living in a maze of hallways and sterile rooms,
not knowing if the person you care most for in the world is alive or
dead or hurting. Knowing only that he's close by, but impossibly
out of reach. Knowing only that your people could be strapped into
some kind of machine that chews them up and spits out bone mush
and sticky sap. It's much better to freeze and bleed a free man.

"After that, I found a Cree family that was on the run too.
They let me camp with them a bit, gave me food and clothes and

information. Told me about small pockets of Anishnaabe still huddled around here and there. Back then there were smaller communities, like the one you lived in. And that's when I met your dad, walking into a settlement by Huron with the Crees."

I felt a sharp jab in my guts at the mention of my father, like a poisonous bubble bursting, one that I'd been trying to protect in the soft wet of my insides.

"I ate real food and slept for a week. Then I began bartering, trading game and knowledge for clothes and camp gear. All I needed was a gun. For that, I had to promise to show your dad and his Council to the capital. They had this crazy notion that there was goodness left, that someone, somewhere, would see just how insane this whole school thing was. That they could dialogue. That they could explain the system had to die and a new one be built in its place. Like that wasn't scarier to those still in the system than all the dreamlessness and desert wastelands in the world.

"I brought them to the borderlands and drew the final roads in. I couldn't walk all the way in with them. I was a fugitive from the school, and I needed to get back. I still had to find Isaac. So your dad, he shook my hand, gave me the rifle, and walked away."

I remembered the way my mother had changed when Dad didn't return. Her skin turned to paper, and on it was written all the worries that'd ever crossed her mind and heart. I saw his back walking away from Miigwans, out of the safety of the woods and into the unknown of the city. And I knew he wouldn't have gone if he hadn't been driven by his love for us, me and Mitch. I was listening with every cell, desperate to pick up a new piece of information or add a new color to the picture that was my father's last days. Of course, Miig had told me this story before, more than once when I bugged him. But it had always ended right here. This time, he continued.

"After that day, I walked back to the school. It took about eleven days, and in every hour of those eleven days I imagined what I would do when I got there. There were murder fantasies and romantic reunions. I imagined snapping necks and then picking up my bae and running into the woods. Of course, it was all bullshit.

"When I got to where the trees thinned into forced meadow, devoid of grass, the air empty of birds, I could barely keep myself from pissing my pants. So, I sat down."

"What?"

"I just sat. I sat there for two days, watching the windowless walls. For what, I'm not sure. I wasn't sure of anything. I didn't even cry. I just sat. I knew damn well there was no way in and not even a window to break in through. What was I going to do? It was a suicide mission that wouldn't get me any closer to Isaac than I was sitting in the woods.

"The morning of the third day, a pickup truck rumbled past me. I waited near the fence gate for it to leave again and jumped in the back, squeezing in between two piles of wooden crates under a blue tarp. I rode along for hours until it stopped on the side of the road and the driver got out to relieve himself. When he was finished zipping up, I snuck up behind him and put the gun to his spine.

"He raised his hands in the air. 'Oh shit. What do you want? Take the truck. Keys are in the ignition.'

"'I don't want the damn truck. I want into the school, and I know you can get me there.'

"He turned then, curiosity getting the better of fear. He took in my appearance, from my shaved head to the gun I held in a steady grip.

"'Dude, what do you want to get into the school for? You're an Indian. Indians go there to die.'

"'What do you mean? Indians go there to get harvested.'

"He shrugged his shoulders and chuckled without mirth. 'What do you think harvesting is? They work them … I mean … you … until there's enough demand built up then they hook you up, and game over, man. It's done.'

"I punched him in the gut, a cheap shot, so angry I couldn't hold it in. The air rushed out of him, and he fell to a knee in his own piss.

"'Where are they? Where in that godforsaken building are the people?' It took him a minute to catch his breath. I wound up to kick him in his side before he put a hand up to stop me.

"'Gone.'

"'What do you mean gone? Where the hell are they?' Then I did kick him. He fell to his side and held both arms up in front to protect his head.

"'They're gone! There's no one there now. Last group was used up. They're waiting on new recruits!' He yelled it at me from behind his arms.

"I paced in a small circle, hands on the back of my head, gun clattering against my skull, then reeled back to the driver, who was still in his defensive curl, eyes closed. 'I don't believe you!'

"He pointed to the truck. 'Check the back.'

"I kicked at his legs, just grazing a shin. 'Don't get smart with me, asshole.'

"'Dude, just look in the back. That's the last of them.'

"I looked behind me at the truck, then back to the prone man. 'Don't move.'

"He lifted both hands in the air in a gesture of surrender

and stayed on the ground.

"Keeping the gun pointed in his direction, I walked back to the truck and lifted the side of the tarp. Just crates. I yanked it off completely and still, only crates. I took two steps back towards the man before he called out, 'Look in the boxes, man. The boxes.'

"I pulled a crate off the top of a stack and dropped it by my feet. I yanked on the top and the nails gave way. Inside were rows of glass tubes, held in a metal rack and cushioned by plastic wrap. 'What the ...'

"I took one out. It was a frosted test tube with the shadow of liquid inside, a thick, viscous liquid that was neither cool nor warm. I turned the tube and on one side there was a paper label.

"'67541B, 23-year-old male, Odawa-Miqmaq.'

"I grabbed another. '46522Y, 64-year-old female, Metis.'

"'No.'

"'67781F, 15-year-old male, Inuit.'

"'No.'

"'66542G, 41-year-old male, Euro-Cree.'

"I didn't think. I didn't consider. I walked back to the driver and started shooting. It wasn't even his fault. He was just a cog in the system. Not that he didn't know what was going on, but still."

We had slowed down. The sun was setting. Miig motioned for Chi-Boy to go ahead to scout the next campsite, then continued.

"I didn't kill him, not right there. I hurt him bad, though, shot him in his arm and a thigh. He was bleeding pretty badly. And crying. He cried hardest when I drove away with his truck, leaving him there all alone. That was the worst part. He pleaded with me to take him, but I was deaf to him then. Not that I wouldn't hear him clearly later when I tried to sleep. I loaded the crate in the back and just drove away with them all, knowing leaving the driver meant he would die slowly and without dignity there on the side of the road."

"What did you do with it? With the dream stuff?" I couldn't help myself, I had to ask.

"I was too late to save Isaac. I took too long. I had to live with that, but I couldn't live with the people being served up like a club sandwich to the dreamless. So I tried to take them home.

"I drove to the lake, one of the last ones I knew still held fish. Got as close as I could from the road and then trekked in, back and forth, one box at a time. Then I camped there for four days. I sang each of them home when I poured them out. It rained, a real good one, too. So I know they made it back."

Chi-Boy looped back and guided us to a swatch of even ground under a ridge of thick pine where we'd spend the night. The group started unloading. I stepped forward to drop my pack and set up, but Miig grabbed my shoulder, holding me there for a moment.

"Thing is, French, sometimes you do things you wouldn't do in another time and place. Sometimes the path in front of you alters. Sometimes it goes through some pretty dark territory. Just make sure it doesn't change the intent of the trip." He put his right hand in the center of my chest. "As long as the intent is good, nothing else matters. Not in these days, son."

ROGAROU COMES HUNTING

WE WERE ON day eight since RiRi, keeping a steady pace with early mornings and late nights, when we were jerked to a stop by Miig. He stood stock-still for a minute, head tilted towards his right shoulder so that his good ear was raised to the tree line.

"Off the trail now. Now!" He chopped the air with his arm, directing us to scatter left into the trees.

We jumped, clearing the taller grasses and crashing into the low-hanging branches with our loaded backs and stacked shoulders. Tree and Zheegwon each had an arm under Minerva's so that she almost floated into the bush, still hanging her head as she had been for the past week. Miig stayed on the trail until we were all off and then slipped in beside us, quickly passing us in near complete silence.

Then I heard them. Sharp, short blasts of fetid breath pushed through a metal cylinder through the scruff of a combed-down moustache. There were two of them, about a half a mile away.

"Fucking Recruiters," Zheegwon said in a loud whisper, and we gained speed and agility at the threat on our heels, jumping a narrow gorge and crossing a clover-filled clearing like gazelles with packsacks.

Miig turned to the right and we followed, tumbling through a dense thicket, coming out the other side into another low clearing with nettles in our hair. We ran until we couldn't hear the whistles anymore, until we'd zigged and zagged our way to what seemed like an untraceable spot. It was nearing dusk when we finally stopped. Minerva was half asleep in the twins' grip, and Chi-Boy had sweat through his outer sweater by then.

"There." Miig pointed with his chin to a dark smudge, only visible through the trees by the geometric slope against the slash of branch and leaf. "It's an old barn. Chi-Boy, come with me to check it out first. We can crash there. They'll be no fire tonight, so walls would be good."

"Frenchie?" Miig said. "Take lookout position there." He pointed at an oak about fifteen feet from where the group was huddled.

I shrugged off my pack and took a run at the trunk. By the time I stopped I was high enough to see over the squatter pines and over the roof of the barn where Miig and Chi-Boy were scouting.

The sky was navy blue in the east, azure overhead, purple bleeding out to a pink-stained orange in the west. The north was black; that was the direction we were headed. The medicine wheel–wearers were down south. The schools were an everspreading network from the south stretching northward, on our heels like a bushfire. Always north. To what end? Now we'd lost RiRi. Now I'd shot a man. Would I even be welcome in the North? I couldn't even protect a little girl. Tears flooded my eyes. I wiped at them furiously with my sleeve. I had to keep a sharp eye. Couldn't lose another one of us.

Miig's fluttery owl call brought me back down to earth. Rose was waiting for me with my roll. "Let's get going. We can't make light tonight, so we need to hurry if we want to get camp settled in the barn."

I took my baggage and unloaded RiRi's off the top of hers to add to my own. We couldn't ditch her stuff, not yet anyway. She rewarded me with a smile that showed a missing tooth on the left side and a dimple on the right cheek. I would have carried a thousand pounds for that.

The barn was empty: not even the leftover scent of manure greeted us. At first it seemed all hollow and singular, but by the last fading light of the moonless sky we caught the outline of a ladder on the far wall. Tree held the base while Zheegwon carefully made his way up, testing each rung with his rubber boot before putting weight on it. Then he disappeared into the darkness.

"There's all soft hay up here! Can we sleep here?" Zheegwon tossed down a few handfuls like confetti.

It was a loft. We each went up the ladder, one by one, plopping into the soft nest of hay.

"Fine, fine, we can stay up here tonight." Miig tried to be stern, but he was already fluffing up a nice soft bundle to lie back on. "But being cut off from the exit's not good idea, so it's early to rise tomorrow, before the sun even, so we can put some more ground between us and them."

"Hey, Miig." It was Wab calling up from below. "Minerva won't come up."

We leaned over the edge to check it out. Sure enough, Minerva stood far back from the ladder, arms across her chest, kerchief tight around her fat face.

"Minerva?"

She just shook her head, not even looking up at Miig.

"Minerva, you okay?"

She nodded, her mouth a thin line.

"You want us to come down?"

We all held our breath. Slopper immediately pretended to be asleep, letting out one fake wavering snore.

"No!" She almost shouted it. "Stay."

We sighed. Slopper's eyes opened.

"Okay, okay." Miig rubbed his chin. "Did you want us to make your bed down there?"

She nodded again and walked to the center of the open barn, pointing at the floor directly in the middle.

"That's not going to be very comfortable, Min," Wab cooed. Her concern was greeted with a grunt and arms re-folded over three layers of sweater. Minerva had been irrational since RiRi's fall. It had been eight days of forced meals, stubbornness, and waves of tears. Even getting her into the bush to relieve herself was an operation in patience.

"All right, then," Miig conceded, swinging his feet over the edge onto the ladder. "Let's get you settled."

Miig and Wab made Minerva a nice bed that night, using two donated sleeping bags from the contented kids in the loft. Miig even had his nighttime smoke down there with her, taking extra-long hauls so she could smudge herself, making shallow cups out of her crepe paper fingers and pulling the smoke over her covered head. I watched for a bit, and at one point she looked up, right at me, and held a single finger to her lips. I was already quiet, so I didn't quite get it, but then again, what was there to get about Minerva?

I kept an eye on the two Elders below, but when Rose accidentally kicked my foot and then left her warm toes against my sole, I lost all sense of anything other than that one patch of skin. Eventually Wab and Miig came up and settled in, and I dozed off to the sounds of genuine sleep from my patchwork family.

I WAS DYING. We were dying. That was the only reason for a noise like this.

Screeeeeeeeeeeeeeeeeeeeeeeeeeeeeee

Sharp metal; angular auditory jabs; cold, dry, biting alarm.

I sat up; seven other heads popped up around me. From close by there was a chaos of singular lights, flashlights bouncing off the trees, shuffling polyester shorts, the squeak of gym sneakers on a wooden floor. And those whistles.

Screeeeeeeeeeeeeeeeeeeeeeeeeeeeeee

I hung my head over the edge and for a moment, in the bounce of a flashlight, I saw Minerva's face, wide awake and without fear. Again she caught my eye and held her finger to her thin lips, just for a split second, before they curled back in a mischievous smile. Then her face was gone, swallowed by the dark. More lights, rushing figures, three of them now, and the shuffle and slide of runners. Miig yanked me face down in the hay. I heard muffled voices as the others were tackled and muzzled in the loft.

"This is for the good of the nation. You'll see, granny," one Recruiter said.

"You are doing a great service, ma'am," said another.

"The world needs you. And, of course, you want to do your part for such a great world," said a third.

Then they turned their beams to the walls, the ceiling, along the floors and into the corners.

"Clear," one Recruiter said.

"Clear," said another.

"Clear," said the third.

Then they dragged out Minerva, who stayed silent, whose smile was the last thing we saw as they turned through the doorway, whom we were sure we would never see again.

We listened to the branches break, the dirt get unsettled, the grasses sway. And from somewhere close by, an engine started up and roared off headed south.

I felt for Rose and pulled her close to me as she sobbed, my own tears caught up in the thick web of her braid.

When we finally convinced ourselves to move, to make the day real, the sky was a cerulean blue with a light gauze of striated clouds. Miig swung his foot over.

"Jesus." He yanked it back.

We watched him with our swollen red eyes, anxious and numb at the same time.

"Damn ladder's gone."

He hung his head over. Chi-Boy joined him. "I don't see it on the ground. Couldn't have fallen or it'd be right there." They turned and locked eyes, understanding the weight of what had happened, taking in that Minerva had moved the ladder sometime in the night, before the Recruiters woke us. Understanding that she'd sacrificed herself and allowed us to remain hidden. How long had she known that they were coming?

"How are we going to get down?" Wab's voice was husky with unshed tears. She rocked herself back and forth on her heels. Since she no longer had RiRi to comfort in these situations, Wab had to face herself, and it made her more fragile.

Slopper threw himself back on a pile of hay, contentedly stretching his back into the softness. "Man, we're stuck."

I had an idea. I grabbed a handful of hay from beside me and threw it over the edge. Then I grabbed another and another, throwing it off as fast as I could. Rose caught on and started kicking it over.

"Hey," Slopper complained. "Quit tossing all our bedding!"

Miig clued in and mimicked Rose's kicking, and others joined in. Slopper sat in the corner hoarding his own pile of hay until Tree explained to him that we could jump off the loft if we had something below to break our fall.

We threw our packs to the ground below and then, one by one, we jumped after them.

When the last body had fallen, we straightened ourselves out and re-shouldered our packs. We stopped at Minerva's bed, rolled up the bags, and folded her faded star blanket. Wab took that one. She unfolded it halfway to tuck RiRi's soft blankie inside and then folded it back over, her grief inside grief like the blankets themselves.

It was Rose who found the jingles. In a small fold of hide were two dozen rolled tin lids. They weren't smooth and uniform like the jingles we'd seen in old pictures, hung from women's dresses, being danced into grand entries at the old powwows when we were safe to make noise. These were rough around the edges from our camp can opener and stamped with expiry dates and some with company names: Campbell's, Heinz. We passed them around, careful not to slice our fingers on their jagged curves.

"But why? Aren't these supposed to make noise?" Slopper was confused. We'd been told over and over that silence was the only way to move out here, the only way to stay alive.

It was Chi-Boy who answered, out of character. "Sometimes you risk everything for a life worth living, even if you're not the one that'll be alive to live it."

We wrapped them back up in the hide we'd found them in, and Rose pushed them into her pack, tears streaming down her dusty cheeks.

Miig left a pinch of his precious tobacco on the spot and mumbled his own goodbye as we shuffled out into the bright new day.

"Well," he said, joining us in our squinty examination of the woods. "North it is."

He turned to start the jog back into the cover of bush. My feet wouldn't move.

"No." I barely recognized my own voice.

The others, slowly following Miig, stopped and turned until finally Miig did as well.

"What's that, French?"

"I said no. I'm not going north."

The rest of my little family looked at me with curiosity. Something had changed. Whether it was this second huge loss or the life I'd taken with all the speed of vengeance back at the cliff, I wasn't sure. But there was no more north in my heart. And I wasn't sure what I meant to do until I said it out loud.

"I'm going after Minerva."

ON THE ROAD

EVERYTHING WAS DIFFERENT. We were faster without our youngest and oldest, but now we were without deep roots, without the acute need to protect and make better. And I had taken up a spot that'd opened up in the middle of it all, somewhere between desperation and resolve.

We'd decided to find the resistance, and we knew there was a pocket of it near Espanola. We needed information to figure out which school Minerva would have been taken to. Chi-Boy and Miig never questioned the plan. We moved the same way as always, Miig as our leader, Chi-Boy as the scout, but now I was with them, helping to shape our path forward. After all, I was the one who had put us here. It was a burden so heavy I could barely sleep at night for lack of breath. What if I was leading us to our deaths? What if we were walking into a place full of more trickster Indians? What if there were no Indians at all? Instead of sleep I counted the stars and kept six on the individual breathing of each remaining member sleeping in their tents around me.

The weather was shifting fast, and you couldn't see your breath anymore, not even in the hour before the sun rose. Miig and I were out collecting water from our tarp traps when we found the first sign that we were getting close.

"French, here." He motioned me over to a thin elm in front of a semicircle of pine. He pointed out a small dent in the side of the trunk. I bent closer and the dent turned into a scar, and then the scar revealed itself to be a series of deliberate cuts.

"What is it?"

Miig ran his fingers over the marks and gave a short laugh. "Huh, I think they're syllabics."

"What's that?"

"That is our written language."

I reached out to feel the language on my skin for the first time since Minerva had breathed her words over my forehead when she thought I was sleeping during her nightly check-ins. An arrow, a line, a couple of dots.

"What does it mean?"

"I don't know syllabics. Isaac was the linguist. But I do know it means there are Nish close by who do." He sounded more hopeful about an impending meeting than I would have imagined, especially after the last one. Maybe he felt something in the tree that I didn't.

The next day we spent taking stock and repacking our gear. We needed to know exactly what we had if we were getting close to Espanola. And we needed to make sure there was nothing unnecessary left in our packs. Speed and agility were the benefits of a tighter group, and we needed both now.

"Hey, French, you want to come with me to look for mushrooms?" It was Rose. Something about her voice made my neck prickle. It had to be her voice because there was nothing exciting about looking for squat fungus in the bush.

"Sure." I tried to play it cool. We didn't have much time to hang out these days, not with the ferocious pace I'd set and the breadth of my self-assigned duties: moodiness, anxiety for the safety of every person, insomnia ...

"S'go then." She motioned to me to follow with a tilt of her head, her long hair loose against her faded grey T-shirt. I got up from where I'd set up by the tent to count and recount ammo and followed her through the pines.

The forest was quiet in here, like a room so full of small voices it hummed with silence. We walked for almost an hour, just listening, enjoying being close to each other without the distraction of the others and the reminder that we were so much less than before.

She stopped short in front of me, and I almost slammed into her back.

"See mushrooms?"

She shook her head. "No. But I smell something."

I opened my nostrils and tried to inhale slowly. She was right: there was something else there, something different in the woods.

"I think it's water." Her voice was a whisper, as if she could startle the water and it would rush off into the denser bush, leaving us behind.

We walked in a small circle, sniffing at the air like dogs. Finally, she chose a direction and we rushed forward.

The trees were dotted with scabs. They sat like blisters on the smooth white of birch. They caught our hair as we passed, combing it across our skin. We left a few strands there, and I was happy in the leaving.

I followed her to the smell of water, ecstatic, almost crazed with hope and the small bundle that was building to a fire in my chest.

She moved ahead, pushing through the dense bush like a coyote. I was seconds behind her, muscles pumping, face smiling, watching her break free and throw arms forward and back in wide strides. She was so beautiful. I wanted to catch her, and I wanted to watch her flee. I could find no satisfaction in my intentions; they were too tiny for the wholeness of her and who I was with her.

I loved her. The certainty of the feeling was clear and bright and brown and lean and it hit me in my throat so that breathing became weeping. And then she screamed from the other side of the trees.

My pace doubled, eyes stinging. I jumped through the bush where she'd disappeared. I was ready to fight, fists already heavy. I was a man then, not a sixteen-year-old too skinny and awkward for real strength. And there she was, breathing so heavy her shoulders heaved up and down. She was standing still in a clearing, and I pulled up beside her, grabbing her elbow both to stop myself and to take measure.

"What? What's wrong?" I could barely breathe. I bent forward, hands on my knees, to catch my breath.

Her voice was high with excitement. "Water. Real water. And I saw a fish right there." She pointed somewhere in the middle where the water tore into frills around rocks.

It was a thin brown brook, pulling itself like a ribbon across the curve cut into the rock just ahead. It didn't rage or wave or crash. It bled from somewhere up the hill and carried itself with quiet grace across the tortured ground, over the glassy rocks, feeding bundles of greens with tenacious roots, some pulled from the split earth and dangling under the cool surface like old ladies dipping vein-bruised legs into a pool.

I fell to my knees, crunching into the early spring crust of leaves and dirt, laughing. It was too much. It was too much. Her and the bundle I carried for her and the water and the bush and everything. Everything made to ache and splinter and seek and throb by the loss of our parents, our homes, our words, our Elder and our RiRi, our safety. I laughed until I was crying, and she moved closer, pulling my head to her legs so that I leaned there at first, then clutched at her. She pushed a slight hand into my hair, brushing the branches and leaves out of its length. I pulled at her legs until she fell to my side, and I reached, taking as much of her as I could in my too-skinny arms, pulling her into my chest, warm from the bundle burning there.

There were sounds now that came from a memory of my uncle. My uncle and his old stereo and his army of battered CDS lined up on the kitchen counter, two stacks of cooking pots as bookends.

He slurred even when he was sober, which was hardly ever. He pointed with palsy-fingers. "Grab one there, boy." He dropped his arm and took a swig from a brown bottle. "And make it a good one, by the Jesus," he growled before taking another swallow.

Mom and Dad were back in the house still, trying to figure out what was going on. They'd sent me and Mitch to our uncle's cabin out by Huron since there were whispers of danger and missing kids. I was young enough to remain silent most of the time. Mitch was old enough to be loud, so Uncle preferred my company. Even now Mitch was running wild with our cousins somewhere outside.

I grabbed a thin plastic case from the middle of the stack, the way Uncle had taught me to choose a card when presented with a fanned-out deck. I hoped this one was the good one he'd asked for. I carried it to where he sat on a low stool with his bottle and belly fighting for room in his lap.

He took another deep gulp and wiped his lips with the back of his hand, setting the empty bottle on the ground by his feet. "Let's see here." He took the CD from my hands and struggled to focus on the cover. "Ho, ho!" He smiled real big, and I released my breath. "Oh boy, you some kinda seer or something?" He lowered his gaze to my face like a lion stooping to smell a daisy. I shook my head.

"I think you must be. This here ..." He held the case up so I could see a bouquet of hands reaching for the sky or each other, on a pink background with white letters behind them. "This here is exactly what we need."

He took two tries to get onto his feet and took a minute to unplug some things and plug in others, and then finally the stereo whirred to life. He deposited the shiny disc, pushed some buttons, and picked his selection, then turned to face me where I'd taken his spot on the stool. He closed his eyes and straightened his back up against the counter and waited for the music to begin. "Pearl Jam. Real tradish, these boys."

It started with an echo turned inside out, and a small yell like a man captured. Then the bottom fell out and he escaped and I tumbled along on his release. Snapping drums, a flexing of sound, and a high threading of guitar over a smoother cadence and then the man sang.

Wrapping up and then throwing off. Wrapping up and then throwing off. The sounds were relentless, and I wiggled a bit on the stool, uncomfortable in its strength.

"Whaddya think, boy?" Uncle yelled over the high whine stacked on deep bottom notes.

I thought for a long while. Long enough for the song to start to spiral back into its first echo, and I answered as honestly as I could manage.

"It sounds like if grey could make noise."

That's what I heard here, now, beside the water with this beautiful girl pulled into the bony shell of my arms. I heard capture and release and a high whine over something that echoed off the trees growing downwards towards the brook like pious monks in all manner of fancy dress, voluminous green silks peeking out of their austere brown habits.

How could anything be as bad as it was when this moment existed in the span of eternity? How could I have fear when this girl would allow me this close? How could anything matter but this small miracle of having someone I could love?

And I kissed her and I kissed her and I didn't stop. I had no way of knowing things would shift again, that I wasn't as alone as I thought after all.

FOUND

FOR THE SECOND time in what seemed to be a very long life, I was woken up by the crash and yell of confrontation just outside my tent.

"Oh, hell no." I jumped up this time, gun already in hand. "Slopper, don't move." I crept to the flap, heard Rose cursing outside, and unzipped it enough to get a one-eyed peek and to push the barrel of the gun out. Instead, a barrel poked in from the outside.

"Shit."

"That's right, boy, I'll be taking that." Someone yanked the zipper up and over the curve, and the flap folded inside. The man, his face covered with a red bandana and dark sunglasses, pulled the gun out of my hands. "Now put your hands right up in the air where I can see them."

I was furious with myself. Disarmed while I was still on my knees. It was like I hadn't learned anything since RiRi. I raised my hands, palms out, to face height and folded myself up and out of the tent. I stood my ground in front of my captor, keeping my gaze narrow and pinned on my reflection in his shades.

He stood tall, and I couldn't be sure if he even bothered to look at me until he said, "That's right. You can give me the evil eye all you want, boy, just keep those hands in the clear."

Still staring, I yelled out, "Chi-Boy?"

"Yeah," he answered from somewhere to my left.

"Everyone okay?"

"Okay. We're all here."

A second man came into view, his face similarly covered, and pulled Slopper out of the tent behind me. The boy grumbled and flopped onto the ground beside me, pulling the second man over with him.

"Jesus, kid. Be careful." This one was female. Hard to tell with the getup they had on, layers of dark clothes and faces covered. The one guarding me laughed a bit.

"Who are you?" I was pleased to hear my voice remain steady.

I got no response except to be pulled by my sweater across the clearing and pushed to sit beside the rest of the group. I saw two more bandana-clad intruders; these two held crossbows at waist height, not really aiming them anywhere, though they were loaded.

Everyone looked to be fine, not tied up or roughed up. Slopper was placed beside me. Our captors stood in front of us, lined up in their bandanas and sunglasses.

"French," Miig called to me from the other end of our lineup. "Remember that carving in the woods?"

"That's enough, old-timer." The female guard kicked at the sole of Miig's shoe.

I looked down the line at him. He pointed at the intruders with his lips.

I raised my eyebrows. These were the people who'd left the carving? The ones who knew the old syllabics system?

He nodded, and we leaned back into our respective places.

I cleared my throat. "I think you're who we've been looking for."

No answer.

"We need help."

One of the figures holding a crossbow snorted. "Don't we all, little cousin. Don't we all."

So Miig was right: they were Indigenous.

"Maybe we can help each other."

The woman answered this time. "We don't need help from anyone. Nobody helps nobody no more. And we certainly don't need help from you. Probably working for the schools. Little snitches, looks like."

I addressed her, shrugging. "How do we look like snitches? Do we have new clothes or good weapons? Are we too well fed?"

She glanced at Slopper, whose shirt hem didn't quite connect with the waistband on his jogging pants.

"Lady, we've seen snitches." I paused, lowering my voice a bit, readying myself to yell it out. "We've killed snitches."

They all looked over at me now. There was no boastful pride in my face. Just five and a half years of hard living.

One of the guys with a crossbow leaned into the female to whisper, and she turned and jogged away from the camp.

Rose shivered against my shoulder, and it was the first time that morning I'd realized she was right beside me. It was warm now, coming on May by Miig's calculations, but the mornings were still bitey and she was in her pajamas — an old T-shirt and a cut pair of long johns. Keeping my eyes on the guard directly in front of me, I slowly raised my arm and placed it over her shoulders, drawing her into me, the other hand still raised at face level. There was no protest from either of them.

"Getting real sick of these mornings," Wab grumbled.

Just then the female jogged back. Behind her, an older man followed. His face was not covered at all, and he was very clearly Nish. In fact, there was something about him that was familiar beyond the general. I flipped through the pile of faces in my memory but couldn't solidly place him. Maybe we'd run into him for a day or a meal out on the road?

"So, who are you then?" He stood in front of us, hands clasped at his back so that his impressive paunch greeted us first. His question wasn't unfriendly.

"Miigwans Kiwenzie, anish de kaz." Miig spoke first, giving him his full name. The man opened his eyes real big.

"Get up, please." Then he gestured to the guards around him. "Help them all up, please. These are our guests, not our prisoners."

"Coulda fooled me." Wab was still bitter as she stood, brushing the grass off the back of her faded sweatpants, the initials of a university she'd never attended stamped across the seat.

"And help them pack up camp. They are joining us for breakfast." He turned on a heel and left the same way he came, without waiting for a reply from any of us.

"What if I don't want to join you for breakfast?" I challenged, stepping into the space between me and the guard who'd disarmed me earlier. I was still sore about that.

He laughed into his bandana and then pulled it down to reveal a smile wide with white teeth. "Come on, little cousin. I'll help you pull up camp. Later on I might even let you have your gun back." He pulled down his hood and revealed a head of long, dark hair, pulled back into a ponytail at the nape of his neck.

I flushed hot. Turned out this guy was not much older than me, and his arrogance was unbearable. "I'm not your cousin." It was all I could manage before he cut me off to address Rose, still at my side.

"Though I'd much rather help you." He gave her one of those big smiles. "But I'm sure you are quite capable."

"I am very capable," she responded before walking back to her own tent. I was a little upset that she hadn't given him more attitude than that.

"We don't need your help at all." I tried to lace my words with poison, but that only made him laugh.

"Suit yourself." He wandered off to chat with his friends, several of whom had also pulled down their bandanas.

"Asshole." It was under my breath, but I still said it.

I packed quickly, shoving and stuffing instead of folding away. I placed bags puffy with chaos by the doused firepit and joined Miig at his site. I rolled up his tent around the pegs while he carefully folded his blankets.

"Who do you think they are?" I didn't bother to whisper; we'd been left largely alone while the intruders chatted by the firepit. I cringed to see the asshole using my tent bag as a seat.

"Not sure yet. But I do know the old guy."

"You do?" I spun around to face him. "Who is it? Did we meet him on the road?"

"No." He was slow to answer. "I can't be sure right now." He was being evasive, and that, on top of being sassed by someone my own age, frustrated me. I left him to finish up and joined Rose, who was now dressed in a pair of jeans and a grey shirt. She had braided her long, curly hair in one thick rope that fell over her shoulder. Even now I couldn't help but notice how beautiful she was.

She saw me and smiled me over to a stump where she'd helped

prepare supper the night before. "You're a mess. Sit down."

My own braid was two days old, and tufts stuck up here and there. She untied the bottom and pulled it apart. I noticed the asshole watching us, a peculiar look on his face like jealousy, and I smirked. She brushed my hair hard and re-braided it for me. Much better than a stupid ponytail like some people. I felt real nishin.

Ready to go now, I followed Miig's lead and walked behind the newcomers into the woods. Despite our recent tragedies, he seemed less stressed about this new development than I was. Though I was still acutely aware of my missing gun.

They walked us through the bush, in a semicircle, and then southeast. After about half an hour we arrived at a tree-lined hill and stopped.

"What the heck? There's not even anything here." Slopper sat on a rock, exhausted and cranky at having to wait for his breakfast this long.

"Look closer, big man." One of the crossbowers clapped his hands, and two bodies in camouflage stepped out of the trees at the base of the hill, bows pointed at us.

"These are the guests, coming to join us," he called out, and they stepped back into the trees. We walked towards the hill, and now I could see a cave carved into it. This is where we went, single file, into the hill itself.

I felt panic when we'd gone through the door, past more guards and into the dark. I thought of RiRi and Minerva then, and aggression filled my limbs like adrenaline. Miig put his hand on my shoulder and I deflated, but only just a bit.

The cave opened into a low, wide room filled on both sides with tents and makeshift abodes of impressive structure: panel walls, blanket doorways. The space was clean and orderly with a hum of activity. Children were gathered in one corner, taking turns reading from a paperback book under the stern eye of an older woman who watched us with a face that revealed no interest as she shushed the children back to work. Some faces appeared in the doorways of the "homes," but they quickly disappeared. We were a quiet sensation.

We were led to the back of the cave and into a smaller tunnel than the entrance, one of four branching off the back wall. I hesitated at the mouth and had to be pushed forward by Rose, who walked behind me. "We're good. All good."

"What if we're not?" I whispered back.

"Nothing we can do about it anyway. There's too many of them."

This was very true. We were kind of screwed if they turned out to be Recruiters, or traders, or some kind of cannibal tribe like the twins' wiindigo people.

She left her hand on the small of my back, and I reached behind to grasp it in mine. I decided right then that I might be okay with dying at this point. I had lived. I recalled the moment we'd found water, and even here, in this tunnel with the potential of being eaten by cannibal Indians still undecided, all the blood rushed away from my head. At first I thought that this was what made my eyes squint, what made them take in too much light. But then I saw we were coming to the end of the path and daylight was up ahead.

We emerged into a valley, surrounded on all sides by high walls of smooth rock. It was about thirty meters in diameter, and the ground was lush. Here the grass and weeds were sharp and thick and grazed our shins. I was so busy looking down and holding onto Rose's hand that I forgot all about being anxious.

Then I smelled it.

Tobacco. Cedar. And the thick curl of something more, something I thought I'd only ever smelled with the memory of smell.

"Holah, that's sweetgrass!" Rose slipped into her old accent, picked up from years with the elderly before she'd come to us.

"We grow sweetgrass here." It was the man from the woods. "That's what you see all around you." He was smiling, patting the tips of the longer strands we stood in.

"Miigwans." He approached us, arms open. "We are so pleased to have you with us. When the Council gets out of the lodge we'll all talk."

I looked back to where he pointed, against the far stone wall. There, at the base, was a squat, round structure, piled with layers of old blankets and tarps. In front of it burned a low fire and two piles: one of wood, the other of round rocks.

"Is that a sweat lodge?" I could barely breathe. An honest-to-God sweat lodge? Here, in this weird valley hidden by stone hills? Where the hell were we?

Then I heard the other word. Council.

"Council?"

Just then the flap on the front of the lodge was opened, a gust of steam poured out and up like a giant's breath, and men started to crawl out. One by one, naked to their briefs, old and young, Native men came out on their knees and stretched back to full height. Each one smiled our way, and Miigwans started to smile back. He smiled so big his eyes almost disappeared in the folds of it.

The last man out of the lodge took an extra minute to stretch out to his full height. He leaned heavily on the man beside him, and I saw that the bottom half of his right leg was missing. I was distracted by it, too distracted to look into his face until he spoke.

"Francis?"

His hair was longer and his face sagged a bit more at his hard jaw, and then there was the missing lower half of his leg. But there he was.

"Dad?"

I crossed the distance between us with my packs still strapped to my back. I don't remember when I pulled them off. All I know is that when I threw myself to the ground and into the circle of his arms I was small again: no baggage, no years in the bush, no murder. I was small and he was huge and everything was okay.

We cried together like that, happy in a way that had no words, until he suddenly pulled back and scanned the group behind me. And I knew what he was looking for. I caught his gaze and shook my head slowly. Then we cried for a different reason.

Time moved slowly and quickly and we didn't care. Eventually we were sitting at a round table on stumps and rocks, all level to the same height. I sat between my father and Miig, who had embraced, as they made introductions between their respective groups.

"This is the Council, what's left of the original one and newer members we've picked up along the way." Dad went clockwise around the table. "Clarence, Cree from the old prairies territory. Mint, Anishnaabe from south in America. Bullet, she's Inuit. Jo-jo is Salish and came to us just last month. This was his introductory sweat we just had, to bring him onto the Council. General is Haudenosaunee and Migmaw. And Rebecca is Ho-Chunk, also from across the border. Seven of us all together."

They were passing around a copper vessel, sharing water that embroidered the outside with beads of cool condensation.

Miig spoke for us. He knew some of the men there but not all. It was different; usually we spoke for ourselves, but I could tell some protocol was set aside. The group was worn out from their sweat, and everyone, not least of all me and Dad, was drained and emotional. He was quick, pointing around the table to our faces with his palm up.

"Chi-Boy, Wab, Rose, Zheegwon and Tree, I'm Miigwans, Slopper, and this is Jean's boy, Frenchie." He paused. "There's eight left."

"Left?" Bullet, who was clearly blind in one eye, turned towards Miig. "You've had some recent losses?"

"Yes, I'm afraid so. Our little girl, RiRi, passed on in the middle of a kidnapping attempt. Damn traders. And our Elder, Minerva, was taken from us by Recruiters."

Bullet's head swung to her right. The older man with the yellowed mustache, General, leaned in to whisper to the small man with the bald head they called Mint.

"What? What is it?" I asked the table.

It was my dad who answered. "We've heard of your Minerva."

"What? Where is she?" Chi-Boy used his seldom-heard voice and sprang from his chair as if he would run to her right that moment.

"That's why we came this way, to try to find her. We thought someone in Espanola or thereabouts would have some idea of which school we could go to to try to find her," Miig explained.

General and Mint whispered again before the older man answered. "She's not in a school. She's here, in town, I mean. In Espanola."

THE MIRACLE OF MINERVA

THE COUNCIL HAD a man on the inside, so their information was good. They told us what they had learned of Minerva after she was taken away from us.

We had been wrong about the marrow, but not about the theft.

Three Recruiters drove an Anishnaabe elder, female, to School #47E, the school closest to the Espanola settlement. She was compliant, jovial even, and Recruiter #1 noted in his log that there might be something fatally wrong with the subject's mind. She hummed on the five-hour drive in and began singing in increasing volume as they processed her: cutting her hair, shaving her skin, scrubbing her body, and preparing her to be hooked up to the conductor. Sensible words — English words — could not be made out, and she refused to answer any questions, not that that was integral to the process. All they needed was to insert the probes, tether the wires, and begin the drain.

Recruiter #2 left halfway through the preparation. He'd been on the job for over a decade and had never encountered someone so "spooky" (in his own words) and suffered nervous twitching that spread to his bowels. He rushed to the washroom on the seventh floor, sadly in a removed area of the building without a local fire escape, sealing his fate in a stall filled with his own anxious stench.

Really, the Recruiters were just there as added sentries at this point. Being at the delicate cerebral stage, it was time for the Headmistress to take over and the Cardinals to carry out the procedure. Recruiter #3 stayed to satisfy his sadistic nature, and Recruiter #1 slouched off to sleep at his desk behind the storage closet with its cages of balls and padding; he didn't find this part interesting. The chase was the crux; after that, who cared how the savages screamed or cried?

The Recruiters would later be identified through dental records.

Minerva hummed and drummed out an old song on her flannel thighs throughout it all. But when the wires were fastened to her own neural connectors, and the probes reached into her heartbeat and instinct, that's when she opened her mouth. That's when she called on her blood memory, her teachings, her ancestors. That's when she brought the whole thing down.

She sang. She sang with volume and pitch and a heartbreaking wail that echoed through her relatives' bones, rattling them in the ground under the school itself. Wave after wave, changing her heartbeat to drum, morphing her singular voice to many, pulling every dream from her own marrow and into her song. And there were words: words in the language that the conductor couldn't process, words the Cardinals couldn't bear, words the wires couldn't transfer.

As it turns out, every dream Minerva had ever dreamed was in the language. It was her gift, her secret, her plan. She'd collected the dreams like bright beads on a string of nights that wound around her each day, every day until this one.

The wires sparked, the probes malfunctioned. Bodies rushed around the room in a flurry of black robes like frantic wings beating against mechanics. The system failed, failed all the way through the complication of mechanics and computers, burning each one down like the pop and sizzle of a string of Christmas lights, shuddered to ruin one by one.

The Council's man on the inside was called to School #47E the day after the incident to take stock and investigate. He noted that several Indigenous people were on site, camping around the edges of the property while it still burned, low now but full of thick smoke, unafraid of the inhabitants and curious as to the cause of destruction. Gossip spread fast.

The school had been imposing: a fallacy of glass and steel against the dusty expanse of the north shore clearing, like a middle finger thrown into the sky, built in record time. Now it was nothing more than one storey, maybe two, of jagged edges, melted poles, and broken cement. A spew of office chairs, smashed computer parts, and chewed-up bricks lay on the ground around it. The fence was mostly thrown down, but the fortified gates still stood.

When the Council's man exited his black vehicle and walked the remaining path to the gate, strewn with debris from the explosions and subsequent fires and maybe even some looting, the campers moved in closer. Soon the road behind him was dotted with spectators following him to the useless gates holding nothing from a broken system, torn down by the words of a dreaming old lady.

The wind shifted so that the heat and smell bore down on the road. And with the Council's man watching, the campers made their hands into shallow cups and pulled the air over their heads and faces, making prayers out of ashes and smoke. Real old-timey.

LOSS

THAT NIGHT WE slept in the clearing. We chose to stay outside. Inside seemed too claustrophobic, and besides, we were more than happy to be close to the lodge.

"Son, plenty of room in my place." I'd helped my dad to his place and had waited in the main living space while he went behind a screen to change and get ready for bed.

His spot backed into a natural corner in the cave so that two of the four walls were stone. The other two had been crafted with a wooden frame hung with wool blankets. The structure had a roof, an old hospital blanket that sealed in the idea of privacy if nothing else. In the space was a cot and a small shelf made from planks of wood separated with cut logs and filled with books, folded clothes, papers, and some braided and bunched herbs. His rosary beads hung from a corner of the shelf, and in between a pile of sweaters and a stack of spineless books was a framed plastic ID card. I went in close, checking that he was still busy behind the screen first.

It was my mother's health card. The green plastic embedded with white letters that spelled out her name: MARY E. DUSOME,

SEX: F, DOB: 03/15/2027, ISSUED: 04/11/2049. The rectangle for her picture was harder to make out. It was dark with age and wear, like she was standing in the shadows even then.

He returned, his eyes half closed even as he spoke, leaning on a carved crutch that curved under his arm like a smooth cradle. The reunion, the sweat, the long day had all taken their toll. He wore a pair of grey sweatpants and a droopy wife beater that showed the sagging skin on his arms and the strength still hard in his chest. It also revealed a series of scars knotted like bark up his side, around to his back, and climbing up his neck into the back of his hairline.

"Nah, I'm okay. Just gonna help the crew with their stuff. Maybe I'll sneak in after?"

He nodded, pulled me in with one ropey arm for another hug, and patted me hard on the back, digging his chin into the crook of my collarbone so that I knew he was working out the reality of my physical presence.

I turned to leave, pausing at the exit. "Dad?"

"Yeah?" He was lowering himself onto a cot.

"Mitch gave himself to them, so that I could get away. Mom, well, Mom couldn't ..."

Dad hung his head, perched on the edge of his cot, knuckles flat against the mattress like a resting gorilla so that his shoulders sat high by his ears. He didn't say anything. It was too much right now.

"Maybe soon we can talk about them, eh?"

"Real soon, French." He kept his face tilted towards the floor. "Real soon."

I was exhausted, but we needed to talk. The others knew it. When I returned they were already sitting at the fire. Someone had thoughtfully helped Slopper with his tent, and he was already passed out inside of it. I could hear his reedy snore through the canvas.

"You staying out here?" Tree seemed surprised, but also a bit relieved.

"Yeah, I'm still a part of this family, aren't I?"

"Yeah," Zheegwon answered. "It's just that you have a real family now."

"Real? What's that supposed to mean? You're not real?" I picked up a stone by my foot. "So this won't hurt, then?" I chucked it at him through the fire.

"Oww, jeez." He rubbed his shin where it had bounced off his shin. "All right, all right, we're real." We laughed.

"So, we need to figure some things out then, I guess." I addressed Miig, who was sitting up very straight, staring into the low flames.

"No, not really." I was surprised by his answer.

"What do you mean?" It was Rose. "Don't we need a plan?"

"Sure we do," he replied. "But the end is the same. We are going to get Minerva. French was led here by that belief, and it turned out to be a good one. Minerva is close by, and he found his dad. That's a pretty overwhelming sign we're on the right path."

I think we expected more hesitation, and maybe a story or seven about what happened at the schools. Not that Miig was weak or cowardly. Not at all. Just that we expected him to be more skeptical, to calm our feverish ambition. To be the voice of stead-fast reason. Instead we found a tired old man and a cooperative soldier all wrapped up in one Indian. It was like he had faded, somehow.

"I just mean the dreams. The words. Don't we need to talk about Minerva finding the key?"

"She didn't find anything. She always had it. Maybe we just need to be better listeners."

I pressed him, "What about strategy? A plan? Shouldn't we be mounting an attack now? While it's dark?"

"This isn't my territory. Tomorrow we can meet with the Council and figure things out from there." He yawned and walked out of the ring of light thrown by the fire. "Right now, I need sleep."

"We're off too." I wasn't sure Tree and his brother had picked up on the subtle shift in Miig. They stood and made their way over to their tent, more in unison when they were tired than any other time. I noticed their cap was on neither head.

Maybe that was it. Maybe we were all just exhausted. It'd been another day on the run, another day being woken up by strangers in our space, and then, at the same time, a day unlike any other we'd had. Hell, I was tired.

Wab started the work of putting out the fire safely, but she had an odd serenity in her movements. Chi-Boy began his usual end-of-the-night patrol. I turned towards the steady drone of Slopper's snore before Rose grabbed my arm, just above the elbow.

"Can you come to my place for a minute?"

The invitation knocked some of my anxiety out of my limbs. I rarely got to spend time with Rose. We were a sad, rushed bunch these days. But the slightest touch and I was right back to being a teenage boy with the biggest crush in the world. I thought maybe it might be more than a crush, what with that afternoon by the river. But I couldn't be sure. Everything was hot and cold and horrifying and hopeful. Terror is an odd bedfellow.

"Sure."

I crawled in the tent after her and was immediately struck by how empty it was. There was one bedroll in the middle of the space.

Against the back wall were her bags, one open with a couple pieces of clothing pulled out. Beside her bed was a small solar-powered lamp that cast a moon glow that didn't quite reach the corners.

In here I could smell the angst and earth and awkward of my own body, and I was embarrassed. I stayed by the door while she crawled to the back wall.

"You okay?"

I wasn't sure I was. "Yeah."

"That's crazy, eh? Finding your dad."

"Yup."

She examined my face for a moment before continuing. "I think Miig is a bit worried."

"About rescuing Minerva?" I started to pull off my sweater. It was warm in here.

"No." She tilted her head in thought. "No, I don't think so. I think it's more about you."

"Me?" I paused, my sweater halfway over my head. "What about me?"

"Well, you've changed."

I was quiet. Had I really changed, after all? I didn't feel changed. I just felt … less. Or maybe it was more. Not changed so much as living at a different volume.

"And I think, even though it's great that we found your dad, well, you know what happens when we find family."

Now she sounded worried. She dropped her beautiful face so that the waves of her hair covered half of it. I wanted so badly to move it aside. I wanted so badly to kiss her again. And I wanted to tell her I wouldn't leave. That I would never leave. But I couldn't.

The memories I carried from the days I'd had with my parents were kept in cradleboards in my mind, situated in complete safety, even the bad ones. In them, there is always this feeling, an understanding more than an emotion, of protection. It didn't matter what was happening in the world, my job was to be Francis. That was all. Just remain myself. And now? Well, now I had a different family to take care of. My job was to hunt, and scout, and build camp, and break camp, to protect the others. I winced even thinking of it. My failure. I'd failed at protecting, and now, as a result, I failed at remaining myself.

Maybe I would stay. Maybe it would be the only way I could keep my sanity, to stay with my dad and inch my way back to Francis.

She made her way, on hands and knees, across her bed and over to me. "I won't ask you to come with us, French. I wouldn't do that to you."

She was right in front of me now, her face an inch from mine. She smelled like sweetgrass and a deeper smoke. Despite the shock of finding my dad, the odd behavior of Miig, the confusion of the new place and how we arrived, the stress of Minerva's impending rescue, all I wanted to do was kiss this girl. So I did.

She didn't pull away, and so I leaned in until we were pushed back onto the layers of blankets that made up her bed. I pulled back to look at her, to make sure she was good. She smiled, grabbed my braid, and brought me back to her.

I can't say how long we were there before the song interrupted us, but when I caught my breath and came out into the bowl of the valley, it was full dark. It was impossible to ignore for a few reasons. For one, any sort of noise could bring the predators, so we tried to stay quiet. And then there was the song itself. That's what sent me out of the tent.

"Do you hear that?" she'd whispered through my hair.

I'd listened. There it was. "Yeah," I'd responded against her neck.

We'd stayed still, just listening to the shake of a dry seed rattle, alert to danger, until the singing began.

Miigwans.

Now I stood near the firepit and set my feet in the direction of his voice. It was a low, moaning voice, the kind the body used to travel through pain, the kind a child uses when they've realized the higher pitched tone used for bringing their mothers isn't working and they are alone after all.

From the back entrance of the cave I saw several guards. They too were listening. But since they stayed there by the doorway, I guessed they weren't too concerned and we weren't in any imminent danger.

I found Miig by the southwest wall. He'd lit a smudge and a candle so that his face was clear in the handful of light and obscured by the handfuls of smoke. I stood back a bit while he sang, knocking his rattle against the air and rocking on his heels where he rested.

It was warmer outside now, and the wind in this valley was minimal. Miig wore a T-shirt and black jeans without the burden of coats, and I was reminded of his life outside of us. The scars from his school stay, the tattoo of a feather below his collarbone, the outline of the buffalo on the back of his hand. His hair was longer than usual, and the sides had grown in so that he seemed younger, less severe. His duct-taped boots were pulled off his feet and placed at the edge of the light where he sat.

I waited until he was done singing, until after he had mumbled some words and smudged himself. I waited still, while he settled into a more relaxed cross-legged position, and even when he packed up his rattle and a docked feather. I waited.

"Well, come here then." He didn't look up as he put away his bundle.

I came into the light and sat opposite him, mimicking his cross-legged pose.

"You still up?" It was an odd question that he didn't mean, since, obviously, I was still up. What he meant was, why was I still up.

"Haven't made it to my tent yet." I meant it to sound nonchalant, but his return smile made me blush.

"Rose must be lonely in that tent by herself."

I squirmed a bit.

"It's okay, boy. All I'm gonna say is babies are the most important thing we have to move ahead. So when they come, they need to come to families that want them and are ready to take responsibility."

"It's not like … I mean, we're not …"

He held up his hand. "Don't worry. No need to explain to me. You're a good man, French. I already know that."

We sat in silence for a minute before I switched gears, the uncomfortable subject making it easier to ask what I really wanted to. "Miig, are you okay?"

"Are any of us okay?"

"No, really." I leaned in to touch his knee. I needed him to know I was serious. "You seem weird since we got here."

"Just since we got here?" He smirked, then waved away his own lightheartedness. "I know what you mean, French." He gathered the edges of his buckskin bundle and tied them off. "Just tired, I guess."

"Yeah, all this running …"

"No, I'm more tired of missing Isaac, is all. Just an old man with an old love, I guess."

All this talk about Minerva and the schools must have brought up a lot of unresolved feelings for him. I thought about him pouring a hundred vials into the ground, one by one, mourning his partner.

"Well." I wasn't sure what to say. "We'll get Minerva. And then we'll shut them down. All of them."

He looked me in the eyes, the first time since I'd sat down. "I know you will, Francis. I know you will."

THE CIRCLE

WE WERE UP early the next day, unsure of where to begin a day
without running. Very quickly, though, the work of the main camp
took over. We spent the morning in assigned chores: gathering
water from the rain barrels to boil, coaxing the small vegetables
in the garden to stay alive, washing clothes, checking the trap
lines. Soon it was lunch and everyone came together in the clearing to eat.

"You guys planning a rescue for your Elder?" Clarence had sat
beside me in a spot where the grass was soft. He was eating dried
meat. I had made him promise earlier to teach me how to dry and
smoke meat so we could keep it longer when the hunt wasn't so
good.

I nodded, not wanting to talk anymore since the asshole from
yesterday had sauntered over. Clarence followed my gaze to the boy.

"This is my nephew, Derrick," he told me. "We travelled
together from out west. He's a good hunter."

By then he was standing in front of us. I had to put my hand
up along my brow to block out the sun to see him. I didn't like

it, looking up at him. I wanted to stand, but didn't want him to think I needed to get up to prove anything.

"The best, Uncle. I'm the best hunter." He smirked and lightly kicked the bottom of Clarence's boot with the toe of his own.

"Yeah, yeah. And he's real humble, too." Clarence laughed. "Derrick, you know Jean's boy, Francis, eh?"

"French," I corrected.

"Yeah, sure, I know Francis. I, ah, escorted him over here yesterday." He made air quotes around the word *escorted*.

"Whatever. Big man with a gun." I decided to ignore him, looking back down at my bowl of salted potatoes. He didn't deserve my attention.

"No, Francis. I'm a big man always. Don't need a gun, though I am capable of using one when I have to."

Clarence cut the boy off. "Okay, Derrick, why don't you get yourself some food over there."

"Yeah, I think I will go get some food, Uncle. I have to check the lines this afternoon. Someone has to feed the women." He stretched out his arm and puffed out his chest before leaving, blocking out the sun so that I was thrown into his shadow.

"Don't mind him. He's just looking for something to rub his antlers on, you know what I mean?" Clarence clapped me on the back. "Plus you have girls in your group. He's just looking to prove himself." He ripped off another hunk of meat and chewed it thoughtfully, looking around the clearing.

Suddenly I wasn't hungry anymore. I swallowed what was in my mouth and excused myself. I handed my bowl off to Slopper and a smaller boy his age named Sam, who were the designated dishwashers for the meal, and wandered over by the lodge, planning to walk the perimeter of the clearing just to check things out.

I still felt uneasy. Maybe I just needed to get a better handle on where we were and what was ahead of us. I sure as hell didn't want to think about where we'd been and what I'd done. And now we were here with his group, and there was this ass who was trying to impress the girls by being a dick to me. What was up with that? I walked at a brisk pace to avoid the others. I needed to think.

"Hey, wait for me." Rose jogged over. Her hair was pulled back in a loose bun that bounced like a pompom on a toque as she ran. I kept walking, a little slower than before.

"Where ya going?" She caught up and walked beside me. "Thanks for waiting, geez."

"Nowhere."

She walked at my pace, swinging her arms and kicking at rocks along the way. I made my way over to where the hill started its incline, dotted with low shrubs and a thin veil of elm trees.

"Well, what are you doing?"

"Nothing."

"Nothing?"

I just nodded, making my way through the bush but still behind the trees so I had a better view of the green bowl of the clearing. Why did things still feel so uncertain even after I'd found my dad? It had been years since I'd even allowed myself the fantasy of imaging he was still alive, and yet here we were, together. And still …

I didn't realize until I had walked a few feet that Rose was no longer with me. I turned and saw her there at the bottom, arms crossed, hip thrown out. "You coming?"

"Well, do you want me to?"

I shrugged. "Up to you."

She unfolded her arms and placed them on her hips. Then she

turned on a heel and stomped away. I shrugged again and walked in the opposite direction.

"TONIGHT'S SOCIAL NIGHT over in the cave." General was visiting with Miigwans when I returned to our group's circle of tents. They were chatting in the last moments of daylight.

General was a pleasant looking man who wore his grey hair at shoulder length and had a neck hung with beaded ropes. He smiled a lot, the kind of smile that went right up into his eyes, and maybe for this reason alone I agreed to follow them over to the cave to check out the festivities. When we got there they were still cleaning up and placing seating in a circle, facing inward towards the center of the space.

I excused myself from the two men and made my way over to my father's room. Since the door was a blanket and the walls were mostly fabric, I knocked on the wooden frame around the draped doorway. "Dad?"

"Come in." He was sitting on his bed, wrapping his damaged leg in a tensor bandage. He smiled when I entered. He was wearing a long undershirt that had been black at one time, but was now faded to grey, and what looked like a pair of tropical print swimming trunks that hung wide on his thighs. His damp hair was freshly cut, and he smelled like good soap. "Boy, I could get used to hearing *Dad* again, let me tell you." He patted the mattress beside him, and I sat down, sighing as I did.

We sat there for a minute, in silence.

"Boy, what's the matter?"

I couldn't answer. Instead I shrugged again, slumping my shoulders after so I could put my elbows on my knees and hold my face in my hands.

"You sure look like something's the matter."

I couldn't answer him because I really wasn't sure what was wrong. On top of that, I felt guilty that I wasn't happier. We'd found Minerva, now all we had to do was get her from the Recruiters. And I'd found my dad after all this time. It was really two miracles in one, and all I could do was feel sad and confused.

Dad finished wrapping his stump and leaned back on his elbows. "French, can you tell me something?"

"Sure, Dad."

"What is it you're hoping to find out here?"

I answered too quickly. "Minerva."

"No, no. I mean, why Minerva?"

I was getting irritated. "What do you mean, why? Because she was taken. I spent the first two years in the bush trying to find Mitch after he was taken. Because that's what we do. We look for each other. Didn't you bother to look for us?" I regretted it as soon as I'd said it.

"I did, son." His voice was low, but calm. "Every day." He rubbed a memory of an injury on the side of his ribs. "No matter what. I didn't set up this camp to be my community, Francis. I brought these people together so that we could find our community. But, eventually, that's what we became in the absence of the other. But it doesn't mean we stop searching."

I didn't understand until he said it that part of my ennui had been resentment. Resentment that my father was out here being all revolutionary while his kids were left with an unstable mother who eventually left us all alone. That I hated him for leaving Mitch to sacrifice himself for me. That I was angry about my childhood left to wither and starve in the woods.

He put an arm around my shoulders and shook me a bit as

he spoke. "No one could have guessed the speed and cruelty of this machine once it started up. No one knew what was coming. If I had, I never would have left that day. I would have taken you and your brother and your ma and run north as fast as I could, while I still had both legs."

I leaned into his side and just lay there for a minute, listening to the pull and thump of his broken heart against my hard head. "I've done things, Dad."

He hummed, low in his chest so that it filled my ear with cotton. "We all have, son." He kissed the top of my head like he used to when I was little, and I felt that good sense of safety once more, even just for a minute.

The blanket at the door was pulled back.

"Hey, you guys coming or what?" A young man I hadn't seen before popped his head into the room, then popped back out. We heard his feet hurry away, and then there was a sound I hadn't heard since I was young — so young that all I remember is the sound and not where I was or who I was with when I heard it. It was the sound of a drum.

They hit the drum tentatively at first, checking for tone and pitch. When we passed the food prep area, I saw Clarence holding it over the homemade element they simmered with, a hole in the dirt ground filled with heated rocks from the fire outside. It was a hand drum, and he held it by the sinew ties crisscrossing the back, tilting it towards the heat to tighten the skin over the front.

We made our way to the circle of seats, and my father took one beside Bullet. I stood on the other side of Dad and looked around. Most of the seats were taken. Half a dozen little kids chased each other in and around the adults, who watched with smiles. Bullet seemed to be the oldest one here, and she couldn't have been

more than sixty-five. There were about fifty people in total, a big
enough group that invisibility the way we enjoyed it was out of
the question. So they had to live differently, carving out communities in the spaces they felt they could defend. It was a precarious
existence, to say the least.

Finally, Clarence walked into the center of the circle, clearing
his throat in sharp breaths. I liked Clarence and was happy to
see him. But then he motioned to someone in the crowd with his
drumstick. I looked over to see Derrick, also holding a drum.

"Dammit."

Even worse, standing beside him was Rose. He smiled at her,
and she returned the smile before he joined his uncle. The cave
darkened as my eyes narrowed. What in the hell was she doing
with that jerk? And why was she smiling so big? I puffed out my
chest a bit, remembering that I still had the longest braids, even
in this larger group. That made me a better Indian, after all.

But then the drumming started. Double beat, high and sweet,
round dance style. Clarence busted a lead and then Derrick joined
in, and damn it all to hell, his voice was amazing. I crossed my
arms, refusing to be impacted. My dad tapped his hand on his
mangled knee and Bullet rocked forward and back to the beat.
A few of the younger adults stood right away and joined hands,
circling the singers in a chain. Some others joined in, and soon
the circle was filled with dancers.

I kept my arms folded when the clapping and hollering started
after that first song. I felt a jealous twitch in my midsection when
Wab and Chi-Boy and Slopper and everyone else for that matter
joined in. The twitch turned into a wrench when Clarence raised
his voice to declare the next one was two-step and Derrick
handed his drum to Tree. That elicited *oohs* and *ahhs* from the

twins, who put their heads together to examine and admire the instrument. It twisted and yanked on my stomach when I saw Derrick weave through the audience to extend a hand towards Rose, who shook her head at first and giggled but who eventually put her hand in his and allowed herself to be led out into the center. And finally, the jealousy turned to full-blown murder stomping about my guts when I saw them dance, hand in hand, around the circle. By the time they were facing me, Derrick looked me straight in the eyes and smiled the biggest smirk of self-satisfaction you ever could imagine.

I turned and left the warmth of the circle, jogging down the corridor and retreating into the dark corner of our camp.

WORD ARRIVES IN BLACK

I WOKE UP early the next morning still in my clothes from the day before. As was my habit, I slung my rifle onto my back before leaving the tent. Before I could stop myself, I crept over to Rose's tent, unzipped the doorway not more than an inch, and peeked inside. She was alone, curled in her fetal sleeping position on her bedroll. I sighed. Thank God.

I tiptoed out of the camp, not wanting to run into anyone yet and have to answer the "where were you last night" or "why'd you storm away" questions.

"Hey, French. Over here." Halfway up the incline of the westward-facing hill Clarence held his hand up above his head to get my attention. He was with Miig and General and a few other men I didn't recognize. They were all wearing shades of green and brown, and two of them had leafy branches stuck through their hats.

I waved and made my way over.

"You gotcher gun on ya?" Clarence shook my hand and nodded at the gun barrel over my shoulder. I nodded.

"All right then, let's go. Hunting day." Miig clapped me on the back and smiled, happy to see me there so early. I didn't want to tell him it had been a fluke. That I'd fallen asleep in fits and spurts and gotten up when I couldn't force my wandering mind to stay stationary anymore.

I spent the day in complete silence, trying to emulate the grace of the older men through the woods. Out here there was water, you could smell it in the air. The more north we got, the more life was left in the woods. I inhaled big.

"Closer you get to the coasts," Clarence whispered, pointing east, west, and then north, "the more water's left that can be drunk. The middle grounds?" He made his hand stiff and made a striking motion. "Nothing. It's like where the bomb landed and the poison's leeched into the banks, everything's gone in all directions till you get further out."

I didn't know what to say. I knew that had been Clarence's traditional territory.

"Sorry," was all I could manage.

If he heard me, he didn't let on. "All we need is the safety to return to our homelands. Then we can start the process of healing."

I was confused. "How can you return home when it's gone? Can't you just heal out here?"

Miig and General gave each other knowing looks, and Clarence was patient in his answer. "I mean we can start healing the land. We have the knowledge, kept through the first round of these blasted schools, from before that, when these visitors first made their way over here like angry children throwing tantrums. When we heal our land, we are healed also." Then he added, "We'll get there. Maybe not soon, but eventually."

A high whistle came through the trees, and General pulled me to the ground with him. I was frantic. Was it the Recruiters? I tried to claw my gun strap to pull the weapon into my hands and to the ready. On the other side of me, Miig turned around and put a finger to his lips, shushing my small noises.

I heard footsteps, a deep echo in the ground, and then branches breaking. Finally, there was silence and then another whistle, this one shorter.

From around me came the sudden sounds of breath, and I realized we'd all been holding ours, then movement, as everyone scrambled to their feet.

"Was it Recruiters?" I asked out loud. "Did they get anyone?

General answered, "No, no, little brother. That was the scouts letting us know they had an animal in sight, one that was the right age to be taken. Sounds like they got it, too."

I coaxed my heart back into normal rhythm and followed the group to where they had, indeed, taken down a good-sized buck. Miig was preparing the ceremony when I got there to send it off in a good way. We allowed the deer to take his dreams with him so he had all the magic he would need to find the next world.

We returned mid-afternoon as heroes. I was more than a little smug, trundling down the hill, helping to maneuver the weight of a full-grown buck on the travois we'd strapped together out of branches and sinew. Even though I'd done nothing but tag along and then panic when the kill was actually made. Still, I was there. I was damn near giddy when I saw the look on Derrick's face as we passed by where he was leg wrestling with his friends. He had his shirt off and tucked into his back pocket, and I couldn't help but notice the definition of his muscles. I flexed under my sweater.

"Uncle, I told you to wake me up," he whined, jogging alongside us to speak.

"I shouldn't have to wake you up. You should be awake and ready like the rest of the men. Like French, here." I tipped an imaginary hat in his direction and watched the color blossom in his cheeks. He stopped following us, and we made our way to the outdoor kitchen near the mouth of the cave.

"Oh, French, that's a beautiful buck." It was Rose. She ran over from the clothes-washing area and put her hand on my arm. It made me shiver, and I had to try real hard to remember why I was angry with her. But once I had that image of her and Derrick the Dink two-stepping right in front of me, I pulled away from her.

"Yeah. Why don't you go watch Derrick wrestle over there." I pointed with my lips. "I'm sure he'd love to have a cheerleader."

Her face fell, and I started to feel flustered. "What are you doing, Francis?" She said it low since there were others around.

"Why don't you just call me French? Only people I respect can call me Francis." I couldn't stop myself. I wasn't even sure how much of this I meant.

She grabbed me by my elbow and led me through the kitchen and around the perimeter of the hill, back over towards our camp. When we reached the first tent I shook loose and she turned on me.

"What in the hell is your problem?" She was only six inches from my face, and I could see anger flash in her dark eyes.

"What do you mean, what's my problem? I'm not the one who's mooning after some jerk with a drum." It was louder than I'd meant it to be, and she flinched.

"You're the jerk around here. You wouldn't even talk to

me yesterday and you expect me to just follow you around or something?" She pursed her lips together when she was done, like she had to struggle to keep back some words.

"Oh, I'm sorry I can't be at your beck and call all the time." I wasn't sure why I'd said it. It's not like she actually expected that. I even screwed up my face and flounced my hands about, as if imitating her snobby behavior. Well, this managed to un-purse her lips.

"You know what, French? You're different. At first I thought it was because of RiRi and Minerva, but no, you're even more different here." Her voice broke on the names a bit, but she took a breath and kept going. "I should just leave. After we find Minerva, I should just go. I don't want to stay around here when you're being such an ass."

I'd regret this next line forever.

"What, and leave your new boyfriend, Derrick, behind? Whatever. Don't expect me to chase after you."

Her eyes filled with tears, and I was ashamed. So ashamed I dropped my head and looked at the ground so that all I saw of her retreat was the movement of her shoes as she took off, sobbing.

I waited until I couldn't hear her, until I was able to move my heavy limbs and drooping head. I couldn't go to my tent. I was scared to be alone in there right now. So I trudged the path back to the cave, past the celebrations in the outdoor kitchen, up the corridor and into my father's room. I flopped face first on his bed and stayed that way until he came in an hour or so later.

He rustled about for a few minutes and then, satisfied that I was awake, began to speak.

"Did I ever tell you about how I ended up in the city?"

I shook my head. I couldn't remember even hearing stories about my dad outside of him being my dad. I hadn't really considered him anything other than that.

"I ran away."

I should have sat up, showed some interest. But I just couldn't.

I heard his calloused palm rub at his moustache, an old habit. The sound made me feel safe and very young.

"Yup. I was thirteen when I decided."

"That young?"

"Uh-huh. I remember that day, too. It had rained in the morning, but the sun came out after lunch." I tilted my head towards his voice, so that I held my face in the palm of one hand, listening.

"Painted wood, when you leave it alone, works itself out. Like it needs to get back to an honest shade. It'll fade blue to skinny green. The church where I went that day, it had rubbed itself grey. It made the birch around it seem real stark by comparison, like bone splinters sticking out of the ground like that."

He settled his weight on the bed beside me and continued. "I remember the old people used to say that the church was a medicine house. I sat there that day on top of my backpack in the aisle between two rows of pews so rough they'd cut your legs if you wore shorts to service and thought, this doesn't look like no medicine house to me. They used to say that men who came in left as something entirely different, something with hands that wouldn't obey natural law and hearts heavy and empty at the same time.

"Me, I needed something to change. Maybe that's why I went out there to that church. Nothing seemed solid to me anymore. Like everything was a drawing of what it was supposed to be, you know? I felt like my hands would pass right through the door when

I showed up. But that day my hands needed to touch something real."

He extended his arthritic fingers out in front of him, throwing shadows over the bedspread.

"That church sat in the woods behind our rec center; it was like a small comma in a long sentence. It was shallow and narrow, not much bigger than the portable where Mrs. Gunther taught English with *Reader's Digest* magazines. When it was used it held about twenty people or so, that's at best — fifteen if the Boire boys were at service. Me, I didn't give a shit about God or the Jesus one way or another. But I knew this would be the last place they'd look. If my mère decided to get up that day, and if she knew me anymore, she might come. I didn't care. She'd be better off talking to the wood bugs outside. She'd get a better response. They wouldn't think up new swears to yell at her or jab her with sticks sharpened by Grandpa's old hunting knife. But then, I might not either. But you never could tell by then ... I couldn't guarantee anything."

His voice sounded far away. I turned so that I was facing him now. He spoke to a spot over my head and nearer to the wall, like this was a story that was written in the space between us.

"The rages came at the weirdest of times then: eating Cheerios, watching music videos, hanging out. A garbage can got set on fire outside the school. I couldn't even tell you for sure it was me." He kind of laughed there, a laugh with no joy in it.

"Then I thought, jeez, what if it isn't my mom that finds me here? The thought made the back of my knees prickle. What if it was one of them in a pickup truck, on a dirt bike, in a shiny government-black car, one hand outstretched, the other hidden behind a back?"

His body went rigid. I read the stress in the veins that popped anxious Braille into his neck. His eyes looked at something I couldn't see. "And what was there even to keep me safe? What, a broken crucifix, maybe? My pocket knife? I was thirteen then, not old enough to fight a grown man. So I did the only thing that came to mind just then, something I'd done only once or twice before when shit got real bad. I got to my knees, pressed my fingers so tight the skin around my bitten nails ached, and prayed. I needed an answer. I prayed and prayed, closing my eyes so tight I saw constellations on my eyelids. And I listened for an answer.

"I listened and I heard a bird. I heard a cricket, and I heard some kids yelling for someone to pass the ball. And then there it was, the answer. It was the smooth swoosh of metal and rubber on the Trans-Canada, tied like a ribbon of tar over the bush. Old Highway 11. So I nodded my thanks to the blind Christ and threw my backpack over one shoulder. I was scared, but more scared of staying. I knew at least on the other side there could be a place, anyplace, where hands couldn't reach."

We were quiet for a minute. He was so still it frightened me. Then he pulled away from wherever he had gone and smiled at me.

"I went to the city after that. Bummed around for a bit, tried to stay away from the cops and then the military when they took over. I found your mom there. She was the most beautiful girl in the world. And mean as dirt when she wanted to be. But not to me."

He smiled real big then. And there was joy in that.

"I was so happy, French. She made me feel like I was impor-tant, like a captain of industry or a scientific genius, and that was just from the look she'd give me when I was doing nothing special at all. It was amazing, really. Now that's medicine. Don't need no damn house to keep it in." He nodded his head, as if convincing me of the truth of it.

Then from out in the cave came the shuffle of feet down the corridor and voices getting louder into the valley.

"Jean, astum!" It was Clarence shouting for my dad. We both stood, and I helped him up and out. I slung my rifle forward as we made our way down the hall and into the valley. Chi-Boy popped out the shadows as if he'd been waiting there all along on a spring.

"They're on the move. Tomorrow." It was an old man in black robes, waving his arms while he shouted, half out of breath.

The sound of air being punched out of a gut came from Miig. He'd come from the kitchen to stand behind me. "Priest," he managed. I raised the rifle so he was in my sight. Chi-Boy rushed towards the man, lowering his shoulder in tackle position.

"French, wait! Chi-Boy!" It was my dad, yelling with his hand up towards us. Chi-Boy stopped his charge midway. "This is Father Carole. He's our guy on the inside."

I lowered the gun and turned instead to brace Miig, who was bent over with his hands on his knees, pale with the shock of seeing a school official.

"Carole has news about Minerva."

The older man sighed his relief and tried again. "They're moving her tomorrow morning. They'll be taking her to the air-strip just west of here to fly her into the Capital."

My heart sank. The Capital? How would we get there on time? "Well, I guess that's it, then." I kicked a rock that skidded to a stop just in front of the priest.

"No, son." Dad was smiling. "That's great news."

I squinted at him. "How do you figure?"

It was Father Carole, confident he wasn't about to be mowed down by a bunch of angry Indians, who answered.

"Because, my dear boy, they must pass right by here on the Trans-Canada to get from Espanola to the airstrip. They'll be bringing her right to us."

LOST AND FOUND AND LOST

WE WERE UP early, before the sun. The Council meeting was fast and heated while we discussed the best way to do this. To their credit, no one even mentioned the possibility of staying out of it, not even old Bullet.

"Let's get these bastards. We get the Elder, we have the key." She was heated.

"We need to organize the families to start a pack-up. We'll have to go into deep hiding after this. They'll come for us for sure, once we initiate a fight." Clarence spoke from experience. Out on the prairies, the Cree had put up a fight. They'd held out for a pretty long time, too, before the armed forces were brought in with drones to pick them off.

We loaded up with every available weapon, mostly bows and arrows pulled taut with young wood and reinforced with repurposed wire. There were a few guns, ours included, some crossbows, and an arsenal of knives. There were nineteen of us without Slopper, who we made stay back to "supervise our pack-up." Each one of our little crew was armed and ready to fight. We had all suffered beyond dignity with the loss of two of our group, and the thought of getting one of them back made us almost unreasonable with motivation.

The mapping was the most important part, since location and surprise were our two biggest assets on this mission. Most of the morning was spent studying the route and picking out the best vantage point to wait.

"They aren't loading up a big convoy. They don't think there's much of a threat. It would be even smaller if they didn't know about the Council," Father Carole had explained before he ran back to his car by the main road and then rushed back to his office in town before he was missed. "But still, their ego is big enough they feel pretty comfortable. Just don't you feel any comfort. Not yet."

Soon enough it was eleven o'clock. The transport convoy was scheduled for noon, so we made our way into the trees.

"French, you need to remember these arseholes will be locked and loaded." My dad pulled me aside as I filed past the Council, whose older or disabled members had lined up to see us off.

"I know, Dad."

"And you remember they don't think of us as humans, just commodities." He cupped his palm at the back of my neck and held me there in his anxious grip.

"I know, Dad."

"You take care, French. Don't break cover. Just disable the drivers and wait for them to abandon the cargo, just like we planned."

"I know."

"I'm serious. Don't go playin' hero and rush out in sight, cause they'll shoot you dead where you stand."

"I'm good, Dad. We know. No one is going to break cover. We stay in the trees and wait for them to leave Minerva."

It took General putting a hand on his shoulder for my dad to release me and let me run into the woods. I turned around at the edge and gave him a little wave. I wish I hadn't. The terror on his face sent needles of adrenaline into my muscles.

We split up close to the road and scrambled into position. Me and Derrick lit into the boughs and found leafy nooks to crouch and lay. The rest of the group lined both sides of the road along a hundred-foot stretch where it narrowed from encroaching bush into a single lane. The plan was to wait for the convoy and shoot out the tires. Then we'd disable the drivers or allow them to run into the woods, at which point we'd tie them up so they couldn't join the ranks that would be sure to follow. It was an hour away from town, so we wouldn't have much time before the cavalry arrived. Then we'd spring Minerva and join the main camp, who would already be on the move to another safe haven, a straight shot north from here. Before I scrambled up to my spot, Miig put his pouch around my neck.

"For safekeeping," he told me. "Just in case. I can't lose this. It cannot go back to the schools. No matter what."

I tucked it into my t-shirt and patted it against my chest, nodding to Miig, then ascended.

Eleven bodies flattened against the ground at the edge of the woods. They were safely out of sight, up on a slight hill from the road. That's where Rose was. I'd made sure of it when she insisted on coming.

"Don't get macho with me. No reason at all for me not to fight." She was cold around me, but too excited about Minerva to unleash any real venom as I protested her involvement in front of the others. I had a feeling it wouldn't be all smiles and playful arm punches later on when she got me alone and let loose.

Miig and the twins joined two of the main campers nearer the road, just before the serrated edge of asphalt began. They were crouched behind an outcropping of rocks, left over from a small avalanche off the hill years before. Chi-Boy had run up the road to the start of the vulnerable curve to scout out the convoy's arrival.

Derrick — with a braid *almost* as long as mine hanging over his neck and dangling like a vine — was in a pine straight across the road from where I was perched in sticky balsam. I caught him watching the girls in the tree line, including Rose, and when he looked over to my side I shot him the finger. To my annoyance, all he did was mime laughter, all theatrical and quiet.

Now we waited.

The trees here were thicker than down the road, which made this spot perfect. They threw their shadows over the road like the plaid of Minerva's favorite skirt. Minerva. I couldn't believe she was on her way to us right now, that we were going to get her back. We had to get her back.

"Once she's on the main highway, there'll be more traffic. Then, in the Capital, well, then she's gone into the maze." Father Carole had spoke candidly before rushing off. "It's now or never, I'm afraid."

Noon approached in a slow crouch, pulling itself along the road, warming the air to honest-to-God spring. The ground was thawed now, and the bellies and knees of those in the woods were damp. The air smelled of mud, and with the abundance of precious water everything with the potential of being green flexed and groaned and desperately began to grow. You could almost hear the leaves opening like reaching fingers, almost feel the trees pulling their posture straight.

A long, low whistle unfurled along the cracked asphalt and landed in my lap, barely audible and then only to those listening. Chi-Boy's signal. I stopped breathing, and the scream of quiet filled my head to bursting.

Then, from a short distance away, came the rumble of a motor, then another, and then the gleam of glass and mirror reflecting the midday sun winked into the horizon.

Here they come.

Everything happened in the blink of an eye for the muscles that brought movement. In the mechanism that drove them, where panic had been woken and fear stalked prey, everything took a thousand years.

There were two vehicles: a dusty red car with blue doors in the front and, twenty feet behind, the white van of our collective nightmare. Father Carole was right: they were cocky. Only two vehicles for the weapon that could bring them all down? I guess they still considered her just another Indian, after all. Mistaking their arrogance for stupidity was our mistake.

They were going about eighty kilometers an hour before they slowed down to take the curve. This was our chance. The archers drew and released, and the road was littered with arrows that flew in a trained arc. Some hit the road like hard rain, one punctured the roof of the red car, and another hit the front tire.

BANG. It blew, and the car skidded side to side before the driver got control. By then a second wave of arrows had been loosed. The side window was shattered, and a second point broke the rubber of the useless tire.

The driver used an elbow to push the smashed glass pane out onto the road.

"Gun!" Tree screamed from his spot, just before the driver shot at him. Hands yanked him down in time, the bullet skidding off the rock and into the gravel with a sharp hiss. The driver took a second shot into the trees. I heard a man's yell, and General slumped to the ground, holding his right shoulder.

My mouth was bone dry. I leveled my rifle on the branch just in front of my face and put the car in my sight. It was almost stopped now, the driver still shooting, the tire wobbling off the rim like a hula hoop. Then I saw the van speed up and try to overtake the car, to get in front and away. Before I could aim, shots rang out from the other side of the road and the van screeched to a halt, the long whine of the horn like a solid alarm.

The driver was hit. I looked up in time to see Derrick lower his gun. He looked over at me, and I recognized that face as the one I'd worn just a few weeks ago. He wouldn't be shooting anymore today. His one lucky shot had put him into retirement.

The horn kept going, long and sharp, covering the sound of the passenger door opening and the slap of hard shoes. A blond woman with a messenger bag flying out by her side dashed into the woods, shooting blindly behind her without turning back to cover her escape. Chi-Boy would be waiting for her just past the first cluster of birch.

Now the archers released another wave, and the driver of the red car didn't have time to back up. He was punctured with a half dozen arrows, some along his arm, the last one cutting through the meat of his neck from one side to the other. He fell onto his side, dead in a pool of his own blood in the curve of the empty passenger seat.

Another man, a Recruiter with his whistle, shorts, and baseball hat, opened the back door and stepped out with his hands raised in the air. I saw his mouth open and close. He was speaking, but we couldn't hear him over the thick shriek of the van's horn.

The twins crawled out from behind their rock with a length of rope, Miig watching their six with his revolver behind them. They scrambled across the road, still crouching a bit in case there was anyone left shooting. When they got within spitting distance of the car, they threw the rope and pretty much lassoed the Recruiter. When his legs snapped together under the rope, he fell over, his sunglasses smashing on the pavement, hat rolling off his head. The twins wound the rope fast and tight and then gave Miig the thumbs-up. Zheegwon snatched the cap off the ground and placed it sideways on his brother's head.

It was done. Chi-Boy ran back from the woods, the female tied at the hands and feet and thrown over his shoulder like a bedroll. Derrick was already jumping the last foot to the ground, and those who had attacked from trees were walking cautiously towards the road.

Before I scrambled down, unused rifle on my back, I sought out Rose, spying her and Wab embracing in the dirt expanse between the woods and the road.

We had done it. The twins, two hats for two heads now, whooped and hollered while they dragged the Recruiter off to the rocky outcropping. A couple of the main campers were already in the trunk of the red car pulling out the spare tire. Vehicles were a valuable coup, even one stuck full of arrows like a metal porcupine.

We all met at the van, gathering around the back doors like little kids. Chi-Boy grabbed the handle and yanked. It wouldn't give.

"Locked." We read his lips since the horn was still going. We must have gotten used to it.

Miig pointed his finger to his chest and then towards the front of the van, and gave the international hand gesture for turning a key. He went to grab it from the ignition.

Tree and Zheegwon swapped hats back and forth. And for the first time, I saw Wab and Chi-Boy for what they were as they stood there, his long arm thrown over her shoulders: a couple. I laughed my relief, knowing Minerva was here — she was actually here.

I cupped my hands over the seam between the two back doors and shouted, "Min? It's us. We've come to get you. It's all nishin now. We're just grabbing the keys."

Suddenly the long drone of the horn stopped, and it was shocking, like the absence of ground at the start of a fall. Then, like punctuation, a gunshot poked a hole in the day and all the air ran out.

I leaned around the side of the van in time to see Miigwans, both arms shoved through the window, struggling. The driver, not dead after all, fought back. Chi-Boy ran to the other side and yanked open the door. The van rocked with fight, then there was a second shot and the van was still.

Miig rushed back with the keys in his hand, fear imprinted between his eyes.

"Are you okay?" I was confused, and searched Miig's torso for signs of blood. Why was he shaking? "Did he shoot you?"

I reached out and pulled his button-up shirt to the side, looking for a hole.

"It wasn't me." He forced key after key into the lock until one slid to the hilt and clicked. "He didn't shoot me."

Miig met my eyes for only a second, but I saw panic there; it stitched into his iris and brought electricity to the surface. He yanked the door open, and she fell into his arms. Obviously, she'd been pushed up against the back doors, waiting for her rescue. He caught her and sank to the ground.

I dropped to my knees beside Miigwans, grabbing at Minerva like a kid, like I never had when we were on the run. I grabbed her hand, placing it under mine and over the hole in her chest. Blood, hot and sticky, gushed out between our fingers. Her thin shirt was already soaked through.

"You're gonna be okay," I lied.

She smiled, patting my hand, comforting me, even now that my distress stemmed from her own peril.

The blood blossomed under my knees like peonies over craggy asphalt. Minerva wore a navy blue jumpsuit. Her hair had been cut short, and I barely recognized her. The lines on her face were deep, the deepest around her eyes. She had no sweaters, no long johns under skirts, no kerchief over her head. But when she opened her mouth to speak, I knew it was her for sure. She leaned in close to Miig and spoke words in the language. They fell softly on his face. They must have been real nice words because he smiled then and closed his eyes so that the tears that welled up were pushed out onto his skin.

Rose was weeping loudly. She dropped hard to the ground and gathered Minerva's head into her lap. "No, no, Nokomis. Don't go. You can't go!" She was shaking, her eyes and hair wild on her face.

"Kiiwen. Kiiwen, promise?" Minerva whispered, and Miig nodded. Miig took her other hand, and she began to sing, low, sweet words depleting breath that wasn't being replaced. I knew she was going. Miig picked up the verse and sang. It was a travelling song. We were frantic but silent. We needed her! We all needed her! She couldn't go. But she was singing her song. She'd already begun.

The whole world stopped for that one moment, for an old lady in a jumpsuit and a weeping man covered in blood and anguish to sing a new sound into the wind, to make sure she left with the dreams so she'd have all the magic she needed.

When she was gone, Miig placed her hand back on her chest and rubbed her arm, smiling. I gently placed her hand on top of the other and stood. Chi-Boy walked to the gathering crowd to give them the news.

But Rose, she couldn't let go. She picked up one of Min's hands now, held it to her cheek like a broken bird.

"Kiiwen," she whispered, rocking her foster grandmother, stroking her forehead with a handful of loose curls at the end of her braid. I stayed beside her so no one would interrupt, doing the only thing I could do right now, allowing her to grieve.

Rose looked up into my face. "Kiiwen. She says, go home."

I looked down at Rose, her beautiful face swollen with tears, holding the old woman's head in her lap, still rocking her, her sticky, bloody hands trying to straighten her shirt and smooth down her cropped hair. Heavy tears blurred my vision. I was looking at Rose from the bottom of a well I couldn't remember falling into. "What?"

"Kiiwen, Frenchie. You must always go home."

KIIWEN

AFTER THAT, WE did what we did best: we ran. A few of the main campers took the vehicles and went ahead with the two school prisoners and the body of Minerva. We all met up in two days' time: the ones who drove, the main campers who'd stayed behind to pack up, and the remainder of the failed rescue crew. We left the prisoners by the side of the road a day in. They had a tin of soup each and a blanket to share, so they'd be fine until rescue, we hoped. We buried Minerva the day after, the Council holding ceremony and prayer, even in the midst of our escape. Before I could stop her, Rose took scissors to her curls. When she was done, her lighter hair bounced into ringlets around her face. She didn't cry. She didn't even seem to notice. She was far away with her grief.

I picked up the scissors when she put them down and cut my own braid off to send with Minerva. Afterwards, Rose, retreating a bit from her reverie, evened out my hair for me so that it hung about an inch below my ears. I hadn't felt so vulnerable since the day Miig had found me, half dead, sick from spoiled supplements, hallucinating.

She kissed me when she was finished, tossing the rough edges of my cut hair into the fire. Our fight back in the valley had dissolved in the thick brew of tragedy, no more than a seasoning that we might pull out later on.

We were broken, an almost unrecognizable bunch of mourners held together by habit and grief and a shared history of survival. But we still had Miig, our leader and Elder all rolled into one now, and we had the new campers and the Council, so we managed to keep putting one foot in front of the other. No one said, "What now?" No one mentioned that we'd lost the key to taking down the schools. If they had, we'd have crumpled where we stood, no longer able to move.

We travelled for ten days before we were ensconced in Precambrian rock and vicious pine. Then the group moved as one machine, setting up the main camp, stringing the woods with traps and alarms. By the end of day two it was as if we'd been there all along. There was even a grey muslin flag hung at half-mast by the bent bough archway into our spot.

My dad surveyed the work, leaning on me for support. "Well, it's not as nice as the last place, but it'll do."

Summer came on quick and merciless in the next two weeks. Wab and Chi-Boy were officially shacked up now. Clarence taught them how to put up a tipi, and that's where they slept. When the heat brought with it summer clothing, it became apparent to all of us that Wab was expecting a baby. The whole camp rejoiced and kept her well fed and cared for. Rose tried to be happy. But mostly she was quiet.

The Council spent a lot of time piecing together the few words and images each of us carried: hello and goodbye in Cree, a story about a girl named Sedna whose fingers made all the animals of the North. They wrote what they could, drew pictures, and made the camp recite what was known for sure. It was Bullet's idea to start a youth council, to start passing on the teachings right away, while they were still relearning themselves. Slopper was tasked with putting that together, and he thrived under the responsibility. He even gave them a name: Miigwanang — feathers. We were desperate to craft more keys, to give shape to the kind of Indians who could not be robbed. It was hard, desperate work. We had to be careful we weren't makings things up, half remembered, half dreamed. We felt inadequate. We felt hollow in places and at certain hours we didn't have names for in our languages.

The day Rose left I had learned how to write "family" in syllabics using ash on a creamy curl of birch bark. I was sitting with the Council during syllabics lessons when she walked by, slow and deliberate, sadness in her gait. She didn't say anything, but I saw the peak of her tent collapse from the cluster where it had stood like a circus pulling up for the next town. I guess I knew it right then; I just didn't want to acknowledge it.

When she appeared in the clearing, all packed up and starting her long, tearful goodbyes, collecting advice and small offerings, I took off and hid in a tangle of pines about fifty meters from the camp. I didn't want to see or hear her leave. I stayed there until the sun started to descend, hating myself every single minute. But what could I do? I had found my home, right? And I couldn't just leave my dad; it would kill him. Leaving to go back on the search would be insanity. No, it was better that we just stuck together and stayed clear of the schools for now, until we figured out our

next move, until maybe we'd gathered up enough odds and ends
to open a door.

But sitting there was torture. I kept having second thoughts
that pushed needles into my feet, and I stood and started to run
back more than once only to stop short and talk myself back to
the pines.

"C'mon, French," I told myself. "You have a good place to live
and you found your dad. There's so much to learn here. What could
going back into the woods possibly do?"

I played with Miig's pouch around my neck to keep me
grounded, pulling on the mud-stained shoelace, fingering the
contents through the hide. I loosed the ties a little and pushed a
finger inside the top, absentmindedly seeking purchase. There
was his tobacco that jabbed under my nail and then something
solid, and today my hands needed to touch something real. I had
to give it back to him. We'd survived the failed ambush, and he
should have it back.

I pulled it off my neck and worked the cinched top open with
both hands. I grabbed what was nestled in there and worked it
out, tapping tobacco crumbs into my palm so as to not lose the
precious flakes.

It was a glass vial, only half full. I spun it between my fingers
and saw a label.

"66542G, 41-year-old male, Euro-Anishnaabe."

This must be the vial he'd IDed as Isaac. I recalled what Miig
used to tell me when I'd first come, when I was nosey enough to
ask unwelcome questions and had tried to pry into the contents
of that bag.

*"It's where I keep my heart. It's too dangerous to keep it in my chest,
what with the sharp edges of bones so easily broken."*

When I came back into the clearing, I knew for sure that she was gone. Everything felt different — smaller and bigger at the same time. As was becoming my habit when I was confused or hurt, I made my way to my dad's. He was living in a four-walled tent with a smaller table and a cot. There were some thin rugs over the dirt floor.

He was sitting at the table, flipping through one of the half dozen books the camp owned. This one was a hardcover by a great woman I had heard quoted at Council named Maracle. Jo-jo had brought it with her from the west, where revolution was sparking along the ragged coast. He didn't seem surprised to see me and kicked out the chair opposite him for me to sit down.

I sank into it and, almost on cue, my eyes filled with water. I swiped at them, but eventually they were too quick for me to keep up. My father watched for a minute and then placed the book on the table in front of him.

He sighed so big his shoulders slumped where they curved out of his faded undershirt, so thin I could follow the angles and ridges of his scars like tattoos under fabric.

"You remember how I told you about me and your mom meeting up in the city? About how happy we were?"

I nodded, and dislodged tears splashed on the wood in front of me.

"Well, I could never shake that feeling of helplessness that'd brought me to the church that day back home. It was always there, like the way a blister reminds you of itself every step.

"Your mom, she was always smarter than me. One day she found me drinking bootleg with a couple of the boys in China-town. I was supposed to be looking for work that day. But your mom, she doesn't yell. She doesn't even get mad."

He paused until I lifted my head and looked at him. He was crying too, already saying goodbye.

"Your mother, she just looks at me real serious and says, 'Jean, running only works if you're moving towards something, not away. Otherwise, you'll never get anywhere.'"

I heard this in my mother's voice as sure as if she had been sitting on the cot behind us, braiding her hair before bed, like she always did when she came to say goodnight to me and Mitch.

"Dad?"

"Yes, son?"

"I have to go."

"I know."

I rose from the table, adrenaline pinching my calves to action, stopping long enough to hug him. And he kissed me on the top of my head, just like he used to when I was little. And I felt safe. Safe enough to leave him.

I rushed out of the tent at full speed, skidded into my camp, and grabbed up all my belongings. I left our tent for Slopper and returned Miig's pouch, hanging it off the center pole in his tent across the fire from ours. There was no time to make my good-byes. I knew they'd understand, sure my dad would explain. Besides, I couldn't bring myself to face Miig with the news of my departure. And I had already lost a few hours and night was falling fast.

I took off running, away from camp, the Council, my family: running towards Rose, who was somewhere beyond the birch-beaded edge of the woods, running towards an idea of home that I wasn't willing to lose, not even if it meant running away from the family I had already found.

"Ahneen."

I almost tripped over my own feet at the sound of her voice. Sure enough, there was Rose, sitting on a log about twenty meters into the bush, her backpack at her feet. Most of her newly shorn curls were piled on top of her head in a messy bun; a few escaped and sat on her forehead like springs.

"Jesus! You startled me."

She chuckled. "Startled? You damn near jumped out of your skin."

"Yeah, well … what are you even doing here?"

Her brow furrowed.

"You know what I mean. I mean, you left hours ago. I thought I was in for an evening run." I stood in front of her, not sure if I should sit, not sure if we were continuing on just yet.

"Yeah, well." She kicked at the dirt between my boots. "Maybe I just wanted to give you a break."

"And what made you so sure I would even follow you?" I nudged the toe of her shoe with mine. She didn't look up, but I could see the edges of a smile creep onto her cheeks. It made her eyes narrow and her forehead smooth like a pulled sheet.

"A hunch, I guess."

"Oh, a hunch, eh?" I bent over, pushing my nose into the mass of curls on her head. I smelled flowers right before they burst out of their green cocoons.

"Yeah." She looked up, turning her face up towards mine. "A hunch. And a lot of hope."

I leaned further in, closing my eyes in anticipation of the bright connection of her lips. Then I heard it.

She placed a hand on my chest, suspending my descent, alerting me that she'd heard it too.

I listened. Runners — quiet and travelling light. I held up three fingers to indicate the number of bodies I heard pushing through the trees. They were too close for us to get a meaningful head start. We'd have to hide instead. I pointed to the ground. Rose slid off the back of the log, snaking a leg behind her and dragging her backpack as she went. I placed two hands on the mossy wood and leapt over, landing on tiptoes and then sinking down. We half burrowed in the soggy leaves, the smell of decay and rebirth clouding around us. Then we waited.

When I heard the first pair of feet stomp by, we kept our heads down. Boots. They were definitely wearing boots and not the mesh runners of the Recruiters. When the second tore by I listened harder. The dull click of a rifle butt hitting a belt. Officers travelled with handguns, not rifles. I peeked over the log.

I recognized the braid flying out behind the third runner as he rushed by, holding his rifle against his side, bandana up over his nose. I stood and called out. "Derrick?"

He turned, slowing to a jog. He pointed in the direction they'd come from. "Unknowns, about five or six of them, half a mile northeast."

Northeast. That's the way we were headed. Rose got to her knees beside me.

"Gonna send out the welcome party." Derrick turned and picked up speed back towards the camp. I sighed, counting the available bodies to go out with the welcome party now that Rose and I were gone. And what if they were hostile? We weren't going to be safe to continue on until we knew what was up. I was trying to find a way to delay Rose when she got to her feet beside me.

"Well, I guess we can wait till tomorrow." She picked up her pack, slung it over a shoulder, and started off on a slow run after Derrick.

"Are you sure?"

She shouted back, "Can't let them go without us, that would just be irresponsible."

I smiled. God, I really liked this girl.

I jumped over the log and took off after her, eager for the excitement of a welcome party expedition, where you didn't know if you'd find blood relatives, poachers, or strangers. Neither of us could imagine that everything would change in just a few hours, including the idea of keys.

LOCKS MEAN NOTHING TO GHOSTS

DERRICK. ROSE. CLARENCE. The twins. Bullet. Me. Seven of us. Miig was considering coming but, at the last minute, decided to stay back.

"You're just as good with that gun as I am. And Clarence and Bullet can track. I'm getting too old for this kind of thing." He settled in with my dad to annotate maps with new information: construction sites, the burnt-out school ...

"All right. I'll leave you old grandpas to it, then," I sassed. "The real warriors will take care of this."

They chuckled as I sauntered away. I smiled, but it was fragile. I felt an acute pessimism at the back of my throat when they were together. How could anyone be so lucky as to have two fathers at this horrible time? Something had to give.

"Last chance, Miig. I'll give you a head start if you need it," I called over my shoulder.

"Nah, you go. There's no adventure out there left for me anymore. I'm done."

We rolled out of camp within the hour. We didn't have much

light left in the day and needed to find them before dark. Leaving it to the next day might mean we'd lose track of them, or worse, they'd discover us first.

What was left of the day was grey and windy. Wind caused problems out here. With so much moisture in the air and loose dirt from both tectonic upheavals and the new species of flora tearing up the topsoil, it was like thin mud being thrown constantly in your face. I was glad for the bandanas we wore.

Soon enough we passed the place I'd found Rose waiting for me in the trees. I turned back now to watch her walking behind me, red printed fabric over her nose and mouth, a rifle slung on her slender back with a sling crafted from repurposed seatbelts. She gave me a thumbs-up and I returned the gesture.

"I hope we find an Elder," Tree said just ahead

"Someone who can help against the schools," Zheegwon finished.

No one could replace Minerva, but we'd be lying if we said finding someone like her wasn't on everybody's minds these days.

Bullet slowed a bit so that we were walking in tandem. She was wearing three shades of denim and an old fedora over cropped hair. "This is your first welcoming party."

I nodded even though it wasn't a question.

"We come in full aggression." She tapped the top of her hat so that it tipped lower on her brow, trying to keep the grit from her good eye.

"But what if there are children in the camp? What if they're friendlies?"

"And what if they're not?" She turned to me slightly. "Better to apologize later than to have to bury a friend. Or worse."

"There's something worse than that?"

"Yeah, not being able to bury them." She tilted her head forward and picked up her pace, passing in front once more.

RiRi's face flashed in front of my eyes. I took a misstep and stumbled over a root, my rifle sliding to my side. I caught it in my hand and readjusted the black paisley swatch over my face. You couldn't let wounds take your focus out here. Soon we were crouched in a line behind a cluster of rock, taking stock of the newcomers.

Four tents, military-style A-frames. A small fire with a metal grate slid overtop where they were cooking beans in a tin pot. One camper was washing up in an old red mop bucket with a crack down the side. He wore his hair in a floppy mullet shot through with silver. Something about his eyes reminded me of Minerva, and I wondered if they were related. My stomach pinched up.

Two black women sat stirring the beans and talking about a shared memory back from the city, about a play where the main actor had been too drunk to recite his lines. With their loose sentence structure and the melodic give and take allowing a team approach to conversation I knew they were Guyanese. After the weather got violent and the islands were battered, the West Indian population here had swollen. They laughed together, and I grew nostalgic for my old life.

There were two other campers standing by one of the tents, and it was them, if I'm honest, that made it easier for us to build aggression before we stormed in. They were having what appeared to be a casual conversation, with a relaxed ease about their posture. Neither of them was armed, and one had a towel wrapped around his head like a turban, having just finished bathing. But it was their paleness that set us on edge. One man had long blonde hair loose across his shoulders. The second, in the turban, had his shirt off, and he was pale except where his sleeves would have ended and the skin was burnt pink.

But no old people.

What to make of this diverse group? We hesitated, swinging between optimism and immediate hate. I wished Miig had come. He always knew what to do. And even when he didn't, he could tell which one of us would have the pitch-perfect instinct for that moment to advise.

It was Derrick who made the call, getting to his feet, pulling his bandana high over the bridge of his nose, stuffing his braid into the back of his shirt. "Frig, let's just go. Day's fading fast."

For once I agreed with him.

We slid from behind the rocks and cut through the trees like moving water, crashing over the camp in ones and twos. I grabbed the mullet guy, who was startled but put up no fight. "Let's go, over to the fire. On your knees."

The women were already on the ground, beans boiling over unattended. They held hands while they lay on their stomachs, Bullet standing over them with a crossbow. "Just relax right there, ladies. Relax and I won't be forced to use this."

Derrick had the long-haired blond man by the back of the neck. He steered him over to the fire and pushed him down hard in the mud near the mullet, who had settled back on his considerable ass by this point.

"Jeez man, watch out, okay? I'm not arguing with you."

"Shut it!" Derrick's eyes were hostile over the horizon of fabric. He pushed the muzzle of his gun into the man's spine, sending him sprawling on his stomach.

"Dude, all right, I'm just gonna stay here, just like this." The man raised his hands above his head and folded them there, seeking reprieve.

"Boy, astum." Clarence had the other man with the pink arms, hands held behind his back, walking over to the group. "Enough now. We, ugh, have to assess first."

He tried to cover up his careless Cree with English. We worked hard to disguise ourselves, especially our Indigeneity, around newcomers.

"Astum?" The man turned his head back towards his captor, eyes wide, mouth opening to speak again.

It was unlike Clarence to be violent, so what happened next was more about his embarrassment over the slip-up than his true nature.

"Never mind, you," he growled, grabbing the man's shoulder and jerking him so violently his towel was knocked off and a shock of dark hair fell over his face. He fell to one knee in the scuffle, landing hard.

"Ow, Jesus!" he hissed.

Rose stamped her foot on the damp ground. "I can't do this."

She helped him to his feet and brought him over to the fire so he could pick rocks out of his bloody knee. He nodded his head at her. "Kinana'skomitin."

Clarence and Derrick exchanged a look. Rose helped the women up next, sitting everyone in a row, one beside the other.

"Are you from the schools?" one of the women asked.

"Are you?" Bullet answered with a question.

"Us? Oh God, no," she scoffed. "We're helping to keep people from the damn schools."

Bullet looked over at the mullet, who was sitting up against a tree trunk, cleaning his nails with a sharp stick.

"And how exactly are you doing that?"

The women explained that they had been nurses at the Sudbury hospital and saw the treatments and "volunteer studies" first-hand. They talked about their first mission, taking children, a brother and sister, out of the program and secreting them away through a series of friends and allies. In the meantime, Clarence had lowered himself to a crouch and was in low conversation with the shirtless man who'd thanked Rose in Cree. He couldn't help himself: Clarence was a curator of Cree. He loved his language the way Minerva had loved us, with pride and an enthusiasm of old potential repurposed.

We stood in silence for a few minutes, weapons still pointed at our prisoners. We waited for Clarence or Bullet to tell us what came next, if we were taking them back with us or leaving them here or ... I didn't really want to think about any other alternative.

"Derrick, Tree, Zheegwon, keep an eye on our guests." Clarence spoke up. He called them guests, so that was a good sign. And he was using our real names out loud, too. The knot of anxiety between my shoulders slackened. "Rose, French, Bullet, a word please."

We walked away from the firepit, over behind the tents, Clarence peering into each one as we passed looking for missed bodies or weapons. We stood in a tight circle. I could tell by her face Bullet was annoyed with our gentle-handedness.

"What do we need to talk about? What we'll serve them for a bedtime snack?"

Clarence waved off her sarcasm. "The shirtless one, one of the two pale men? He's Cree."

"Are you certain? It's not all that difficult for a Recruiter to learn one of our languages. He could have just started speaking it when he heard you use it first." Bullet was sharp.

Clarence sighed, kicking a rock by his foot. "I know, that's on me. But I am certain. He's speaking an old Cree I don't even fully know. He's way more fluent than me or anyone else I've met. And walked his lineage back."

"And what about the others? There's only one Native in the bunch, besides this Cree in disguise." Bullet was still skeptical.

"They're allies, real allies. They put their lives on the line. It's not just talk. You heard them," Clarence insisted. "There may be ..."

"Wait," Rose cut him off. "Is he as fluent as Minerva was?" I saw right away where she was headed, so I stated the obvious.

"But he's not old. I mean, not Elder kind of old."

"Why does he have to be old?" She was excited now. I could see it flashing in her dark eyes like the clouds of fireflies that made summer nights frantic with light. "The key doesn't have to be old, the language already is."

We stood there for a minute. The wrinkles in Bullet's forehead smoothed out like a sheet pulled tight.

"Clarence?" I said. "I need to ask him something. Then we'll know."

He nodded. I walked back to the fire, grabbing a red-checkered shirt from a low branch by the last tent. The twins were standing over the nurses and the Nish, their guns pointed towards the ground. Derrick was watching the two men. He kept his rifle trained on the small space between their heads. I put my hand on his shoulder and squeezed, letting him know I had this.

I threw the shirt to the man Clarence had spoken to. He nodded gratitude and pulled it on, buttoning the front over his damp skin.

"How do you dream?"

He looked up, and it wasn't so hard to see his nation there. It was there in his light eyes, the way they angled down and avoided roundness just slightly. It was in the right corners of his high cheeks and the smooth flatness of his lips. It was there in the question he posed back with just the movement of his eyebrows.

"I mean, what does it sound like?"

"Come again?

I sighed. I hoped he wasn't in a mood to stall. "What language do you dream in?"

He smiled, and his lips parted to show rows of bright teeth. I already knew what he was going to say.

"Nehiyawok, big man."

I watched the word leave his mouth, felt it fall over my face through the cotton damp with breath and mud. It raised the skin on my arms to bumps.

"I dream in Cree."

I looked back over to the small council and nodded, smiling.

"Pack 'em up," Clarence called out.

WE WERE GETTING close now, passing the log once more. I slowed down, hoping to walk with Rose the remainder of the trip. Instead I ended up beside the Cree. He smiled, so I tried to make small talk, now that we were able to tuck our aggressive bravado away. Even Bullet had softened, smiling at the back of the line while the nurses laughed and teased each other.

"So, how long have you been in the bush?"

"Oh, years. Too long."

"Were you always with these people?"

"I've been with Talia and Helene, the nurses, since the beginning. They're the ones who helped me get out of the school. I was brought in to their hospital for blood work to determine my eligibility. And, well, here we are." He put air quotes around *eligibility*.

"What do you mean, eligibility?"

He pushed air out his nose and smiled full of bitterness. "To make sure my blood wasn't too mixed. Can't catch a break for being a half-breed, any way you look at it."

I stayed silent. My family didn't really have those problems. No one mistook us for anything other than what we were. I wondered if we were lucky or not. My family, my stolen family.

"How did you stay alive in there?" My voice betrayed the small sliver of hope sliding under my skin. "I heard it's pretty grim."

"I had somewhere I needed to be." He pushed back the hair from his forehead. "Someone I needed to be with ..."

And that's when I saw it, the dark lines curving from his middle knuckle, rounding the ridges of vein, settling just under the cuff of his plaid sleeve. A tattoo of a buffalo on the back of his hand.

"Isaac?"

His eyes grew wide. He dropped his hair so that it swung back into his face, and his feet slowed.

"How do you know my name?"

That bundle I carried in my chest, the one that inflated when I heard about our triumphs, the one that ached with our losses, the same place where my love for Rose nested and the painful memories were enshrined and mourned: from there came the push, and I set off running.

"French! Hey, what's the matter?" Tree yelled after me.

I couldn't answer. I had to get to Miig now.

The moon was hoisted to the center of the sky as I ran, a big stage spotlight among the smaller bulbs of stars. It illuminated the green expanse between trees and the rocky outcroppings that marked the start of our camp. The grass here was waist high with clusters of sleepy blooms nodding their heavy heads in the blue light. I ran into the clearing, pulled my breath in to yell. It burned all the way down my throat into my belly.

"Miigwans!"

A crow, startled by my small commotion, alighted from a branch to the right, cawing his displeasure, a staccato of anxiety stitching the night a darker blue.

A short silence was followed by the quick shuffle of feet and the bouncing strobe of flashlights in hands. A small group came into view from the denser pines by the rock. I bent in two, hands on knees, gasping for the air to call Miig to me, to us.

"Miigwans!"

The group spoke low amongst themselves, and there was movement. I raised a hand to block out the glare and saw Miig pushing through the bodies to the front of the group. "French?"

I laughed out the next ragged breath. I didn't know I was crying until I closed my eyes and the water dropped onto my cheeks, hitting the backs of my hands.

He took a step towards me, then stopped and shone his flashlight into the trees. There was crashing behind me as the others caught up. I turned my head, still bent over to catch my breath, expecting Derrick or quick Bullet. But it was him. It was Isaac at the head of the party.

He slowed to a walk now, the welcoming party and newcomers falling in behind. He slowed all his movements, as if focusing his eyes and reconciling what they saw took motion from his muscles. I heard a sound like an echo turned inside out, and then Miig, who had been standing still, trying to see, to understand, under the blue smoke of moonlight, finally took a step forward.

"Miigwans? Is that you?" Isaac's words jumped up his throat like heartbeats, each bookended with a pause then settling in the grass like blood coagulating. We couldn't move for it. I couldn't breathe.

Miig opened his mouth. The movement unhinged his legs and he fell to his knees, knocking down the grass like so much chaff. He held his hands out, palms turning upwards in a slow ballet of bone, marrow intact after all this time, under the crowded sky, against the broken ground.

"Isaac?"

I heard it in his voice as Miigwans began to weep. I watched it in the steps that pulled Isaac, the man who dreamed in Cree, home to his love. The love who'd carried him against the rib and breath and hurt of his chest as ceremony in a glass vial. And I understood that as long as there are dreamers left, there will never be want for a dream. And I understood just what we would do for each other, just what we would do for the ebb and pull of the dream, the bigger dream that held us all.

Anything.

Everything.

ACKNOWLEDGEMENTS

I sincerely want to thank the arts councils who continue to support the literary arts: the Canada Council for the Arts, Ontario Arts Council, and the Toronto Arts Council. Without their support I wouldn't have been able to take the time to finish this book.

My gratitude to Wenzdae Brewster for taking the cover image and to Michael Snake for being the cover model. It means so much to have such amazing Indigenous youth be a part of this project, chi miigwetch!

I am indebted to the Banff Centre of the Arts for its solitude and landscapes, to my traditional territory of the Georgian Bay for its family and magic, and to the Ontario powwow trail for its laughter and the understanding that we are community even in transit.

I need to thank the Aunties and Uncles who provide knowledge and guidance with such generosity. Among them, Janine Manning, June Taylor, Stephanie Pangowish, Josh Smoke, and so many others.

There are moments when excellence and enthusiasm align and the very best of the best are accessible. I have been lucky enough to encounter 3 such individuals on this project: my editor Barry Jowett, Cormorant visionary Marc Côté, and the ever-powerful Lee Maracle. I am in awe of your skill, your diligence and the belief you had in both me and this book.

To my husband Shaun, and my children Jacyob, Wenzdae and Lydea, thank you for giving me space, time and the support necessary to write. I appreciate your sacrifice and know that I missed you every time I shut the office door to dream this dream. I love you beyond words, and I have a lot of them.

I have so much gratitude for my parents who allowed me to chase the words all through my life until they could be corralled into books. And for making sure that every year, without fail and no matter how much it might inconvenience or stretch our means, I went back home to our community to spend summers with my grandmother, her sisters and a thousand cousins. Because you had the foresight to raise me with our stories and within our territory, I was able to chase these words into this particular book more than any other. This is the best gift I have ever been given.

For my brother Jay and my cousin Chris. Thanks for being halfbreeds with me — running around the Bay, playing euchre with our Mere, pushing through the bad shit together because we knew we came from royalty; jigging in the dirt, fishing off the borrowed dock, returning bottles for popsicles, making soup out of bones kind of royalty.

And finally, as always, for my Mere, Edna Dusome, who kept the stories, raised the babies, shouldered the weight, and laughed all the way to the end.